C000103293

The
Heron

The
Heron

Ibrahim Aslan

Translated by
Elliott Colla

The American University in Cairo Press

Cairo • New York

First published in 2005 by
The American University in Cairo Press
113 Sharia Kasr el Aini, Cairo, Egypt
420 Fifth Avenue, New York, NY 10018
www.aucpress.com

Dar el Kutub No. 2829/05
ISBN-10: 977 424 929 1
ISBN-13: 978 977 424 929 7

2 3 4 5 6   12 11 10 09 08 07 06

Designed by Sarah Rifky/AUC Press Design Center
Printed in Egypt

Translator's
Introduction

SINCE ITS PUBLICATION in 1983, *The Heron* has enjoyed a remarkable reputation that belies its slim profile, and for good reason: readers can enjoy it in so many different ways. As a work of modern Egyptian fiction, *The Heron* draws upon, and overturns, the conventions and themes developed by canonical urban writers like Naguib Mahfouz and Yusuf Idris. As a work of Arabic literature, it resonates with the classics, from the popular carnivalesque of the *1001 Nights* to the philosophical sobriety of *Kalila and Dimna*. In fact, the title of Aslan's novel derives from a character in the latter work: the heron who teaches the pigeon how to trick the fox, only to fall victim to one of the fox's schemes himself. Shades of the heron appear in the novel's character, Yusif al-Naggar, who sees clearly how the weak are set upon by the powerful, and knows (theoretically at least) how to escape their traps, yet is unable to act to save himself. As an account of the Cairo Bread Riots of

January 1977, the novel documents a bloody turning point in modern Egyptian history.

The novel's prominent place in Egyptian letters is even more remarkable given the fact that it is set in an unlikely literary location: a crowded slum on Cairo's periphery. Indeed, it is difficult to appreciate the novel without considering the history of its setting, the neighborhood of Imbaba, itself the creation of Cairo's haphazard urban development. The neighborhood—which remained for much of the twentieth century a largely agricultural area—figures only liminally in Cairo's urban cultures. For one, it lies miles from downtown on the West bank of the Nile. Yet Imbaba stands opposite one of Cairo's richest neighborhoods, Zamalek. Like the south bank of the Thames in Shakespeare's London, Imbaba was once a place of entertainment, and escape from polite society. During the 1930s, the part of the neighborhood that bordered the Nile became famous for the floating nightclubs and bars that entertained not only the British soldiers stationed there, but partying elites and royalty. That neighborhood, Kit Kat, is still known after one of the more infamous cabarets from the colonial period, the Kit Kat Club.

Throughout its history, Imbaba has retained its peripheral status in relation to modern Cairo. While Cairo's roads and transit lines connect to Imbaba, its electrical, water, and sewage networks only partially do. As when this novel was published, Imbaba lacks the basic municipal institutions—such as hospitals and schools—found in most central neighborhoods. Yet, like other slums, Imbaba has no lack of cafés and mosques, both of which figure large in *The Heron*. By the 1990s, these two male-dominated gathering places pushed Imbaba from the edges to the center of Cairene culture. On the one hand, there were the writers, products of Kit Kat cafés, who had established themselves on Egypt's scene. Following Aslan, they wrote not of genteel Cairo nor of historic (if decrepit) Islamic Cairo, but instead experimented with the voices of people living difficult lives in colorless slums. Yet these writers were soon overshadowed by the graduates of Imbaba's mosques. By the early 1990s, Islamists—many recently returned from fighting a Holy War in Afghanistan—had effectively taken over sections of Imbaba, turning them into feifdoms controlled by self-proclaimed amirs who, while attempting to establish the rule of Islamic law, pressed women to change their dress, persecuted local Christians, and harassed the occasional, timid police patrol. Following a spate of bombings in 1992, the Egyptian government cracked down on the 'Emirates of Imbaba,' declaring an emergency and dispatching troops to occupy the neighborhood. Again, Imbaba seemed to be both at the center of Cairo's modern social history and outside its mainstream altogether.

The Heron comments saliently on many crucial elements of this modern history. It describes the effects of the dismantling of popular economic policies—such as subsidies (on staple commodities) and import substitution (as in the steel industry)—associated not just with the Nasserist state, but with national independence itself. It tells the story of the intense market gaming that attended Sadat's Open Door *(infitah)* economic policies and that created class divisions between Egypt's rich and poor that had not been seen since the colonial period. The novel is filled with stories of speculation and black-market trading in everything from real estate and construction materials to flour and sugar. In telling these stories, it gives context to the story of the popular uprising—the widespread, violent protests of January 1977—against Sadat's *infitah* and the IMF austerity programs that accompanied it.

It is impossible, though, to read this novel simply as stories about events, because in Aslan's fiction there is a give-and-take relationship between stories and characters. Stories cannot be separated from the characters who tell them nor from those who listen. Aslan does not make this easy, however, since his characters walk on and off stage at a dizzying pace, and he polishes the features of some to a luster while leaving others in the rough. As you will soon discover, this novel contains some of the most memorable characters of modern Egyptian literature, including most especially the blind, hash-smoking con-man Sheikh Hosni, whose misadventures figure prominently in the film adaption (entitled *Kit Kat*), directed by Daoud Abdel Sayyid and starring Mahmoud Abdel Aziz.

One theme that brings characters and events together in the novel is that of seizing the moment. There are the thuggish maallims who seize upon the opportunities created by the *infitah*. There are the youths—and older men—who grab at sexual opportunities as they appear to come by. And there is the character of Yusif, who ruminates on his failure to capture the opportunities of revolution, writing, and romance. This theme is developed around the novel's many kinds of fish and fishermen. The neighborhood in which the novel takes place is not only located on the banks of the Nile but is also itself filled with big fish who swallow little fish without a thought. And of course, there is also the figure of the heron, the bird that hunts by waiting patiently on the bank only to spring into action when fish swim by. At one point late in the novel, Yusif is fishing and reflects, "Among all the possible signals, the true and the false, there's only one signal on the float: the moment the fish forgets itself, the moment when the fish understands everything, the moment the bite and the cork and your eye and your hand all become one." The passage is not merely about fishing technique. When read against the uprising stirring around Yusif's character, the scene seems to allegorize the matter of popular struggle against state tyranny. In this sense, *The Heron* is a crucial part of the critique leveled at the Egyptian left for its failure to capture the moment of 1977. Yusif is one of the first characters to witness the rebellion but, although sympathetic, he chooses to get drunk instead of participating. He is like the heron in the novel's epigraph who is paralyzed by grief when his stream dries up.

Aslan's novel is hilarious, and my translation, sadly, too often fails the standard set by the original in this regard. Aslan's wicked sense of humor derives from his telegraphic turns of phrase, and he creates his characters and stories in a patchwork that combines the registers of literary and newspaper Arabic with others from colloquial Egyptian and local street argot. In a single sentence, for instance, we might find one clause that parodies the absurd passive voice of Egypt's state newspapers, a second that mimics the formal pretensions of café intellectuals, and a third that conveys the precision of a pimp's curses. In grappling with these aspects of Aslan's language, I have relied on the skills and advice of many friends, most especially Hosam Aboul-Ela and Gamal Eid. Without their help and patience I could not have finished this translation.

The
Heron

They say you sit near the waters of streams and creeks and that if these waters were to dry up, grief would overwhelm you, and you'd fall silent, mournful. . . .

Chapter
One

YESTERDAY IT RAINED. It poured. In the narrow alleys, even the doorsteps of the buildings were flooded. But today it stopped altogether. And, even though the sun remained hidden all day long, the air was warmer. A while ago, evening arrived early.

In the outer room overlooking the small courtyard, Yusif al-Naggar threw the blankets off his legs and sat up on the couch, covering his thigh with the edge of the gallabiya. His father's gallabiya. Behind the curtain patterned with tiny pale flowers, the window was closed. The twilight trickled through the pebbled glass pane of the closed wooden door.

Reaching his hand toward the large cup of warm tea, Yusif al-Naggar got out of bed.

Chapter
Two

WHEN FARUQ'S MOTHER saw him return, wearing his gallabiya and carrying his fishing pole, she turned her head. Walking into his bedroom, he told her not to wake him because he was tired. She rose and took the bag of fish and emptied it into a pan and brought out the cooking sheet. She began to prepare a handful of bran and a bowl of water mixed with salt, pepper, garlic, and cumin and followed after him. She glanced at him lying on the couch and asked him for matches. To stop her from going through his pants pockets, he got up and gave her a box. As she left the room she mentioned that Amm Migahid had died.

Faruq sat up on the couch and asked, "How?"

"People said the authorities found him dead inside his shop," she remarked from the doorway. "They thought he was sleeping, but . . . it turned out he was dead." Then, while stepping out the door, she added, "The cops arrested Amm Omran because they found him sitting there with Amm Migahid after he died."

Faruq got up, put on his slippers and left the house. He crossed the yard and stood under the leaning wooden balcony. Looking at Amm Migahid's shop, he saw that it was empty and barred shut. He reflected for a moment then turned to go talk with Gaber the grocer.

The walls of Yusif's room overflowed with rows of books packed onto wooden shelves hanging from braided cords attached at the sides. There were also two large pictures next to the window. The one hanging on the wall by a small metal clip was a reproduction of the Mona Lisa. The other was hung on the right, over the end of the couch on which he sat. A piece of yellowing paper with a picture drawn on it in India ink hung in a wide, glassless frame whose golden shine, now dulled, looked more like chased brass.

This second picture portrayed an old mule ridden by a man armed with a long lance, a shield on his back. Nearer to the ground, on the back of an unruly donkey loaded with two saddlebags, was his attendant, a round face gazing from below at the noble knight sitting mutely. The background was composed of a group of scratches, and completed by Picasso's signature and a date. On this background, a series of windmills, like small children's toys, were scattered among the legs of the mule and the donkey. The sun hung in the picture's sky as if it were a distorted, cracked ring emitting rays in long, narrow lines. In the room there was also an old pellet rifle, an assortment of empty whisky bottles, cups, pencils, a steel helmet filled with medicine boxes and books of matches, a desk, a heavy mirror with a decorated frame, and a small wardrobe with a record player on top and two pairs of shoes underneath. Behind the door, clothes hung on a small brass clothes hook.

Chapter
Three

FROM AMONG THE books and the magazines piled on the desk, Yusif grabbed his watch. He went out to the main room carrying his large teacup, now empty. The large chair in the room was also empty. One of the children slept on the nearby couch. A young woman stood in front of the basin between the kitchen and the bathroom while his mother sat on the other couch next to the wide window. Yusif announced that he was going to the café. He heard the voice of his mother and answered "Good bye" while going down the steps leading to the yard.

"Good evening, Ustaz Yusif!"

"Hi Faruq."

Gaber handed Yusif a packet of cigarettes. When he had taken them and turned away, Faruq told him that Amm Migahid had died. Yusif stopped and looked at Faruq who continued, "It's the truth. We just got back from the graveyard at Sidi Omar where we buried him. I just got home, changed my clothes, and came right back out. What a chore! All day long pushing and pulling, digging up and down. I said to myself, 'How about a couple bottles of beer on the way home so I can get some sleep?' Why don't you have some with us?"

Yusif thanked him and offered him a cigarette. Faruq took one and lit it. As Yusif left the alley Faruq followed him with his eyes and smiled.

That morning, Yusif's mother told him that at dawn the police found Amm Migahid dead inside his shop. Yusif knew the shop well: black as coal, bare except for a long, ragged mattress and a stove which burned all night under the large brass kettle in which he boiled the ful. Its door was left half shut until Amm Migahid rose in the morning to sell ful to the children.

When Yusif dressed, he thought of Amm Omran. He had been a real friend to Amm Migahid. Whenever Yusif saw the two of them, they were chatting inside the shop. He and some of the others knew that Amm Migahid was the only one who dared to criticize Amm Omran for wearing pajamas all the time. Amm Migahid seemed older than anybody he had ever come across because he was so feeble and hunched. Likewise, Amm Omran was very old, white-haired, a little fat, and always sickly. During the summer, his skin would appear ruddy and smooth and his face would shine like a child's. But now that it was winter, his appearance was just the opposite.

Yusif was thinking that he had to be more careful. Only yesterday Salim Farag Hanafi told him, laughing all the while, that his sister had seen Yusif talking to himself while walking in public. He must have been talking to himself since no one was with him. Just then he saw Amir Awadullah sitting in the entrance of the café. Yusif shook his hand and noticed Amm Omran sitting inside. He wanted to go sit with him, to console him and to get some idea of how Amm Migahid's death would affect him. But Amir brought him over a seat and ordered a cup of tea for him.

The café was nearly empty at that hour.

To the left of the café's entrance, Qasim Effendi was reading something aloud from al-Ahram, while Abdullah the waiter stood listening to him. Abdullah's thin frame was bent over, his hands rested in the fold of his apron, and he squinted through feeble eyes. Two seats away from them, Maallim Ramadan sat dozing next to Sheikh Hosni who, wearing an old gallabiya and an open vest, his coarse hair smudged with whiteness, had planted his heel and began to tap the ground with the ball of his foot to the old Muhammad Abd al-Wahab song, *al-Gondol*, coming over the radio. Two seats away, there was a low glass counter with two bowls on top, one of which contained a number of copper tokens. Behind the counter and underneath a shelf with a large wooden radio, Maallim's seat rested on an empty, overturned case of soft drink bottles. In the heart of the café, behind the marble wall with the two crescents that formed the ring emblem around the name 'Awadullah,' there were the smaller hand-held water pipes with shiny brass necks neatly arranged next to the glass hookah pipes, their hoses covered in velvet with colored, faux-ivory mouthpieces. Abd al-Nabi, the gimp, stood behind the counter in front of the large brazier, lighting the coals and fanning them with a feather fan. To the right, directly in front of Qasim Effendi, Sulayman Jr. was watching four men playing dominoes for money out of the corner of his eye. Gamal, the shoeshiner, left his box under the seat, came over to them, and began to watch them in silence. Empty, ashen soft drink boxes sat in the corner, above them a long, rust-eaten mirror. And just beneath this mirror, next to the empty refrigerator, Amm Omran sat alone, wearing his famous pajamas and matching cap, made of striped cotton flannel. He stared directly ahead, his toothless mouth shut tight.

Chapter
Four

SHEIKH HOSNI RAISED his head and clapped his hands to get some service. But Abdullah the waiter, standing next to Qasim Effendi and listening to him, continued to ignore the Sheikh.

Sheikh Hosni kept his head up, and when Abdullah returned and passed in front of him, the Sheikh reached out and grabbed the edge of the waiter's apron, pulling him closer. When he knew that Abdullah was next to him, Sheikh Hosni whispered "Pay attention, eh!" Sheikh Genid was due to stop by at any moment.

Abdullah couldn't help smiling because Sheikh Hosni, despite being completely blind, had somehow discerned and nabbed him as he passed by carrying his customers' drinks. Abdullah recomposed himself, saying that he hadn't forgotten. There was nothing to worry about, but he didn't want to be involved any longer. "My friend, I'm through with that line of work." He added that Sheikh Genid, unlike the previous sheikhs, seemed to be a respectable man. Abdullah ground his teeth, muttering his disbelief at Sheikh Hosni. Surely the sheikh knew that the café was as much as lost already. Astonishing. The sheikh must also know that he himself was the one most responsible for this loss. In the very near future, God willing, Sheikh Hosni wouldn't be waiting in the café for Sheikh Genid or anyone else for that matter. "I wish that was all there was to it. It says in Qasim Effendi's *al-Ahram* that the owner of the

9

café—and the cinema and the bookstore and Husayn's fish shop and Hagg Hanafi's milk store and the mosque, in fact, the owner of all of Kit Kat Square—turns out to be some foreigner. He's alive and well and is going to sue in court."

Abdullah tried to free his apron, but the sheikh wouldn't let him go. The sheikh listened until the last word, comforting him all the while about the way matters were developing. The sheikh told him to pay attention, to stop talking about this business, and to cancel his tea since he was going to help Maallim Ramadan eat his oranges.

The Blindhunter

For the purposes of enhancing his income and entertainment, Abdullah the waiter had agreed, for a fee, to play the role of scout for Sheikh Hosni.

He didn't have to do anything except, whenever he spotted a blind man, tell the Sheikh what he observed. With time, Abdullah came to perform his job with expertise, providing answers to some of the absolutely necessary questions: the age of the 'customer,' what he was wearing, distinguishing features. He would do this and then back off, leaving everything to Sheikh Hosni who headed over to the blind man and put himself directly in the other's path. The sheikh would ask the blind man if he needed any assistance—where was he trying to go?— then he would take the other by the hand and help him off the curb. All the while, the sheikh let the other believe that he was in the company of a man who could see. Almost always, it took only a few moments for a new friendship to start up between the two and by then, the sheikh would have already dragged him into the café.

No matter the economic circumstances of this friend, a coin or two would quickly find its way into Sheikh Hosni's hand and he'd be off to Haram, the hashish dealer. In those days the sheikh's wife would take his salary at the beginning of each month directly from the secretary of the Imbaba-Ismailia Primary School where Sheikh Hosni worked as a music teacher. She wouldn't leave her husband anything but the little he needed to keep a supply of cigarettes.

How numerous were the blind men for whom the sheikh provided services and found suitable jobs! How often he managed to collect donations from them! How many of these there were compared to the very few who caught on and managed to escape! Or compared to the fewer still who began to suspect—or who got wise to the game—yet stayed on, trying to discover what the sheikh really wanted, and only fled at the first sign of real danger! Of those who didn't realize what he wanted until after they had lost all their money, half blamed only themselves, thinking that it wasn't really very smart for a blind man to hand over everything to any seeing person he just happened to meet on the street. The other half would ask directions to the sheikh's house with the idea of confronting him. After finding the place, they would continue to walk the path between the café and the house diligently and patiently. Determined and alert, then it would dawn on them that, surprise! Sheikh Hosni was just as blind as they were. Ashamed, the swindled blind men fled, never to set foot near Imbaba again.

Whenever he scored, the sheikh would remember Abdullah the waiter: a pinch of hashish or tobacco, a dinner sometimes at Husayn's fish restaurant, some oranges, a fat tip when he paid for his drinks, and whatever else there might be by way of profits. For his part, Abdullah not only would keep the secret, but was also responsible for setting up appointments between the sheikh and his 'friends.' When the time came, he had to watch the street closely. No sooner would Abdullah see the blind friend approaching than he'd let the sheikh know, by some means or other. The sheikh would then stand in the doorway as if he were a man who had seen his blind friend coming and got up to welcome him at the entrance. The sheikh would greet him and drag him along through the crowd and then sit the blind man down beside him. This would take place under the peripheral supervision of Abdullah so that the sheikh wouldn't screw up and greet any old person he bumped into, because that would create complications.

Together, they'd seen good days and bad ones, with the bad seeming to go on forever. Years went by in which it seemed that the world had lost all its blind men except for Sheikh Hosni himself. Abdullah would be on the verge of forgetting the whole game, then a day would come along when he'd go out to the doorway of the café and see an unaccompanied, blind sheikh approaching through the square. Abdullah would retreat quietly, unnoticed, and tell Sheikh Hosni about what he'd just observed. The blind man would have hardly stopped under the tall camphor tree when Sheikh Hosni would run into him with his arms stretched out and catch his sightless prey.

Usta Qadri, 'English,' approached the Khalid ibn al-Walid mosque and hid himself behind the wall. He raised his head a bit so that he could watch from afar.

He was able to see Amir Awadullah sitting by himself in the entrance to the café, just as he was able to make out one of Qasim Effendi's thighs sticking up, resting on his other leg. He recognized the Effendi's black pants. They couldn't belong to anybody else. Likewise, he recognized Abdullah the waiter. The Usta stood there until he caught sight of Sulayman Jr. crossing the street and stopping to talk with Sgt. Abd al-Hamid, the cigarette vendor, who sat with his back to the square under the old stone lamp post. While he stared at the two men, he noticed Maallim Ramadan exiting the café and heading in his direction. Usta Qadri disappeared behind the mosque and retreated quickly across the square to the bus stop and began to look out from there. He didn't relax until he saw Ramadan standing in front of Hilawa, the orange vendor. When Usta Qadri saw Ramadan carrying a bag and holding his change, he wheeled around and ran back to his spot at the corner of the mosque. Once again, he looked up and followed Ramadan with his eyes. Ramadan had returned to the café entrance and was shaking the hand of Amir Awadullah and a friend standing next to him. It was Yusif, the son of Muhammad Effendi al-Naggar.

Chapter
Five

IT WAS WELL known that Maallim Sobhi, the poultry vendor, had purchased Hagg Muhammad Musa's building in which the café was located. What wasn't common knowledge was that he had paid the tenants of the upper floors a bribe to get them to look elsewhere for a place to live. Yusif al-Naggar didn't know the first floor tenants, but in the summer, when he and his companions brought their chairs over to the mosque wall, he could see an older woman and a young woman on the second floor balcony. He could also make out articles of women's clothing hanging on the clothesline. Amir Awadullah was especially interested in this whole matter since the café had originally been rented to his dearly departed father, Hagg Awadullah, and had remained so, officially at least, until this day. Amir clarified the situation for Yusif by telling him that Maallim Sobhi, the poultry vendor, wanted to demolish the old building so that he could build a huge new one in its place. He also spilled the beans about Maallim Atiya, the present tenant of the café, and how over the past few months he'd been taking 'incentive' money from Maallim Sobhi, telling Sobhi that he'd leave the café but then not going through with his promise to clear out. Maallim Sobhi had given up on Maallim Atiya and had started to demolish the interior of the building, ripping out the doors and windows, pulling up the toilets and tearing down the staircase. Sobhi had a government committee come out to the building and convinced them that the old place was unfit for anyone to live in. For his part, Maallim Atiya also knew how to deal with the committee: by the end, this committee decided that although the building was unsuitable for human 'habitation,' it was fine for the café to continue to operate in it. Atiya went back to taking Sobhi's 'incentive' money on the pretense that it would pay for relocating the café, promising that he'd leave the building at the first of the following month, and never doing it. At least, not until after he'd amassed a large sum.

Amir Awadullah said that although the content of this story was familiar, its particular form was uncommon. Then he added that everything changed after the afternoon prayer one day.

Contrary to his habit, Maallim Atiya had gone to urinate in the alley that cut between the café and the poultry shop. Without his noticing, one of the boys who worked for Sobhi approached like he needed to piss too. When Atiya undid his belt and lowered his pants, the young man slashed his exposed side with a sharp knife and fled. According to Amir, Maallim Atiya decided to clear out only after receiving this last 'incentive.'

At just that moment Atiya was sitting in the steel warehouse with Maallim Sobhi and two others trying to hammer out a final agreement. Awadullah said he was going to find out what was going on and asked Yusif not to leave before he got back. Yusif al-Naggar looked at his watch and said he could only stay another half hour since he had an engagement downtown. Maallim Ramadan walked up, carrying a bag of oranges. He shook hands with Awadullah and Yusif. He smiled and squinted, saying, "Pardon me." Rearranging his crotch, he walked into the café.

Maallim Ramadan Takes His Share of Oranges

Maallim Ramadan headed left and gave the bag to Sheikh Hosni, announcing that it was full of oranges. He told the sheikh he could divide them up for himself to be sure he wouldn't be cheated. Gathering up his gallabiya under his big paunch, Ramadan sat down and turned his smiling face. When he saw Qasim reading the paper and Abdullah in front of him standing silently, his smile widened and he turned to look at the sheikh. The sheikh had pulled the bag to his concave chest and dangled his big face into the top. He had taken off one of his worn-out shoes, showing the world his blackened little toes. Maallim Ramadan raised his eyebrow and ground his teeth saying, "Hurry up, old man!"

Sheikh Hosni raised a hand in front of his empty eye sockets, "Don't put out your hands. Spread your gallabiya over your lap right where you're sitting."

Pulling up his chair and raising the bottom of his gallabiya with both hands, Maallim Ramadan replied, "My lap's ready."

The sheikh waited a bit, stretched his hand into the bag and picked out an orange. Saying, "One for me," he placed it in his lap. Then he took out another, "One for you," and threw it on the Maallim's lap. He took a third one out and nodded, "One for me. Isn't that right, Amm?"

Looking at the lone orange in the lap of his gallabiya Ramadan replied, "That is correct."

The procedure of dividing the oranges continued until Sheikh Hosni said, "That's all," threw the empty bag to the side, and gathered his share of the oranges in the front of his old gallabiya. A single, rather large orange remained in his hand. He walked off a little way and began to eat it, asking out loud, "I wonder what Qasim's been reading since this morning?"

The Maallim looked at the four oranges sitting in the gallabiya spread wide over his lap. He looked at Sheikh Hosni's orange-stuffed gallabiya and couldn't figure it out. He tried to remember how the oranges had been divided, but got confused. He was sure that Sheikh Hosni had been saying "One for me and one for you" all along. The Maallim found the whole thing exceedingly strange. He wanted to figure out what had happened. He knew he was angry at the sheikh, but he couldn't understand why. Suddenly, he stood up and lifted the hem of his gallabiya over his long underwear to hide the evidence of what had just transpired. Ignoring Abd al-Khaliq, the undertaker, who was just entering the café, Maallim Ramadan headed over to the gang who worked as trainers in the exclusive Gezira Athletic Club. They came to play dominos with their hard-earned money. He sat watching the game, peeling his orange, trying to forget what had just happened. But he couldn't get it out of his mind. His belly began to tremble and he smiled to himself saying that the sheikh was a bastard, nothing but a goddamn devil. . . . He wanted to let his frustration burst out, but instead exploded with a chortling snort of laughter. He stretched his head out between the players and wiped the tears from his eyes, showin them all the crown of his balding head. At that point, the players jerked back angrily, each one clutching his domino pieces tightly and hiding them from his neighbors. They remained like that until the Maallim noticed that they'd stopped playing. When he saw the look in their eyes, he tried hard to stop laughing. He wanted to apologize, or at least to tell them what had made him cackle so hysterically. He was on the verge of explaining when he suddenly stopped himself and growled, "God! What's with you boys? Can't we laugh?"

Angrily, he jumped out of his seat and the three oranges fell from his lap. Blind with rage, he rushed to kick them out of sight under the chairs. He headed to Murad Street where he plopped his short, full frame at the entrance to his shop. His crimson face looked as if he'd just finished crying his guts out. Usta Sayyid Tilib, the barber, left his shop next door and stood with his white disheveled hair, long sideburns, and small, tanned face. He sat down by Maallim Ramadan who commented, "Those domino-playing Effendis are nasty sons of bitches. They're cold-blooded and heartless."

When Usta Sayyid asked him what was the matter, Ramadan told him all about what had happened with the Gezira Club clique, but he failed to mention the story about Sheikh Hosni and the oranges. Usta Sayyid listened to him, smiling, his legs crossed. This was his usual way of doing things, even if the Maallim wasn't aware of it. Whenever someone spoke to him while he was standing, he listened to the other person while a look of deep sadness began to surface in his sharp features. However, if someone happened to speak to him while he was sitting, whether on a chair or couch, he would listen, drape one leg over the other, and smile without exposing his gold crown. Then his thin mustache would droop as unsettling signs of contentment appeared in his face. Though Usta Sayyid wasn't originally from Imbaba, he was an old friend of the gang. He worked in the barbershop of Usta Badawi behind Kit Kat and lived at the intersection of Qatr al-Nada and Fadlallah Osman Streets with his mother who came from the countryside. He arrived in Imbaba some time ago and rented the shop space next to Maallim Ramadan's fitir shop. He told Qasim Effendi, who got his hair cut at Badawi's, that he was going to continue working there until he finished fixing up his own shop. He wanted it to be 'just so.'

He began to spend his evenings in front of the space he rented, hanging out with Abu Faruq who owned the feed store. Then he moved next door and got to know Maallim Ramadan, Sheikh Hosni, Abd al-Khaliq, the undertaker, Usta Qadri and the rest of the bunch. When it got cold, Sheikh Hosni suggested that they move their evenings indoors, into the empty shop. Usta Sayyid welcomed the idea, and they began to spend their evenings in the shop space, calling it 'the spot.' With time, they furnished it with a mat and empty flour bags to sit on. They also installed a small stove, a large water pipe made of yellow brass, and brought in a basket of coals and a heap of maassil tobacco boxes.

They would enter the shop and, once inside, lower the metal door behind them, leaving only a small opening for ventilation underneath. Then, they'd rig a steel bar from the inside so that no one would be able to open the door from outside. They didn't light any lamps but would sit instead illuminated by the glow of the stove and the big radio dial. In moments of clarity, Usta Sayyid felt troubled, contemplating how the hell he'd managed to bring his mother here all the way from Gharbiya province. Or how he'd left all his relatives in order to work in Usta Badawi's shop behind Kit Kat Square. And he thought about how he'd learnt the trade, rented the spot whose preparations to make it 'just so' hadn't been complete until after the Revolution of '52 took place and the old aristocratic titles were supposedly abrogated. He was amazed at all that had gone into his getting married six times. Now he took to badgering women while sitting in front of the spot. Whenever he saw an attractive woman, he'd abandon his shop and run home. His mother would see him and understand what he was after, she'd tell his wife to drop whatever she was doing and go see what it was that the Usta needed. Locking himself inside his room, he would undress—the image of the woman never leaving his mind—and sleep with his wife. Then he'd go back to his place in front of the spot.

As soon as he caught sight of Nour, Sheikh Hosni's wife, and heard about what she was like, he stopped desiring other women altogether, that is, until Nour died while still in her prime. That white temptress.

During his six marriages, Usta Sayyid failed to produce any children. But that didn't bother him. Like he used to say: he never divorced a single one of his wives for that reason. He loved them all and enjoyed the intimate relations of marriage with each one. Yet, when he stopped having sex with them, for some reason they would die. Then he'd go marry another. Seven years had passed since his mother died, and he'd come to love his last wife Luwahiz very, very much. He would elaborate on that theme when he drank, saying that he could not stop talking with her when he was at home. Sometimes he even kept talking to her while he squatted on the toilet. Then he'd grow quiet and think about this; it was so mysterious, he couldn't think of anything that distinguished her from the other women with whom he'd shared 'the intimate relations of marriage.' She wasn't the most beautiful, nor the most responsive, and she was not knowledgeable about things in bed, or anything else for that matter. In fact, he often wanted to smash her head in with a clog.

Yet, he eventually realized she was going to be the one wife who'd outlive him. He would get out of bed soon after noon prayers, eat a bite, and, in the afternoon, go down to the spot to work, drink tea, and smoke cigarettes. Later, he would head over to Awadullah's café and wouldn't return home until it was late. There, he'd find Luwahiz waiting for him and they'd eat together, sitting on the sofa next to the high open window. And they'd talk and look at the trees by the bank of the river and watch the eastern side of Kit Kat Square until Sheikh Hamada al-Abiad performed the dawn call to prayer from al-Sunniya Mosque. Then they'd go to bed. In the last few years, he had begun to attend the final nights of some of the mulids. This began with the mulid of Sidi Hasan Abu Tartur, Sidi Ismail al-Imbabi, Sayyida Zaynab and Sayyida Nafisa, and ended with the mulids of al-Sayyid al-Badawi and Sidi Ibrahim al-Disuqi.

Usta Sayyid wore a white gallabiya and wanted to become a dervish. He started to go to the memorial services of any recently departed person. Strangely though, he could no longer stand to let Abd al-Khaliq, the undertaker, touch him; indeed, he'd grown to hate the very sight of him. Abd al-Khaliq knew this and tried to comfort Usta Sayyid, telling him that he would give him special treatment when he died. He promised to wash him thoroughly and cut his fingernails. Also, he said he would be careful so as not to disturb him when he plugged his orifices with cotton. He'd do all that extra service even though Usta Sayyid would only be a corpse and no longer able to feel a thing.

Maallim Ramadan smiled and his natural color returned to his face. He realized he was still holding the orange he'd peeled in the café, so he broke it into halves, offering one to Usta Sayyid, pushing on the Usta's shoulder to shake him out of a trance. Usta Sayyid came to, looked at the orange half and saw Maallim Ramadan's face. He flatly refused the orange and said that all he wanted to do was to go to the café to find out what was happening with Amm Migahid's memorial service. Maallim Ramadan nodded his head in agreement, swallowing what was in his mouth so that he wouldn't gag if he laughed suddenly. He told Usta Sayyid to go on ahead, adding that when he finished eating the orange he'd walk over there as well. He looked at Usta Sayyid's face and said that he'd just left Abd al-Khaliq, the undertaker, who was going to perform the necessary tasks, at the café, "In other words, don't worry about a thing. Go over there and you'll find Abd al-Khaliq sitting there, waiting for you. He'll already have everything arranged."

Usta Sayyid didn't bother to respond. He just looked down in disgust at the face of Maallim Ramadan who began to shake with laughter and said, "Really! I swear didn't mean anything by it! And anyway, our lives are in the hands of God."

Usta Sayyid shook his head and opened the door with its tall glass pane. Turning his back on Ramadan, he cursed him silently, then asked God for forgiveness and kept on walking until he drew close to the café entrance. There, he saw Sheikh Hosni leaving with another blind man who had been coming around to visit him these days. Usta Sayyid considered the sheikh to be a piece of garbage, the person more responsible for his personal suffering than anyone else. For that reason, he stopped in his tracks and watched the sheikh leading his blind companion toward the bank of the river. Usta Sayyid spat and cursed Sheikh Hosni. And when he thought to ask God's forgiveness, he said to himself, "Around here, one could go on and on forever just asking for forgiveness."

The Two Sheikhs

Truth be told, Sheikh Hosni never actually said that he could see. However, he did imply it. From the very first moment, his behavior around Sheikh Genid was that of a seeing man. He would ask the other to step up or down or to turn this way or that in order to avoid a hole or piece of pavement. He would stop along their way and greet the people he saw and knew. He would stir his friend's tea, describe women to him, and interrupt him, pretending to look at his watch and say what time it was.

Sheikh Genid had rejoiced at this blossoming friendship and considered it a blessing from God. After eating the orange, he was completely taken by that strange, colorful world which Sheikh Hosni presented to him while leading him down the bank of the Nile. Sheikh Hosni, for his part, was nervous since he knew that a long time had passed since he'd practiced this vocation. In the past, if he accidentally did something only a blind man would do, he could correct his mistakes by saying any old line and playing dumb. But he couldn't do that with Sheikh Genid. "Look, he's a nice guy. He's a pious man and we're on intimate terms. His only fault is that he's got no sense of humor. His jokes fall flat on their face. Because Sheikh Genid was so earnest, Sheikh Hosni had to be very precise about everything. He was really more concerned about it than he needed to be and was especially defensive about the fact that everybody called him Sheikh Hosni in front of Sheikh Genid. He went out of his way to explain, as clearly as possible, the reason why they called him Sheikh so that Sheikh Genid wouldn't become suspicious.

In order to get rid of any doubts there might have been around this issue, Sheikh Hosni began to tell the story of how when his father saw young Hosni, he got confused and enrolled him in Sheikh Muhammad Qutb's religious school over on Murad Street in order to learn the Qur'an by heart. Despite the fact that the blind man and one-eyed man are not equals ("neither are the rich and the poor, the tall and the short and so on"), everybody continued to call him 'Sheikh' Hosni and never by any other title. And when asked about the secret behind this treatment, he explained that they called him by the name of his grandfather, who was the first one to come to Imbaba and the one who planted the tall camphor tree, "You know that tree we met under the first time? That's the one!" He added that he hated this title of sheikh which didn't befit him at all, then quickly tried to rectify his mistake so as not to hurt Sheikh Genid's feelings. The story he invented was that in Imbaba the esteemed title of 'Sheikh' did not imply that he who carried it would, with time, be counted among such righteous men of God as Sheikh Genid. Absolutely not. This word, in Imbaba, meant that the person it described would end up, invariably and no matter his social position, becoming a lowly Qur'anic reciter in the graveyard of Sidi Hasan Abu Tartur. For that reason, he hated the word and refused to wear a turban or jubba and from that day forward Sheikh Hosni was useless outside the creative arts. Owing to the persistence and strength of will he'd inherited from his mother, he was able to escape the fate of graveyard reciter. He was silent for a moment then suddenly said, "Even Dr. Taha Husayn himself never had to overcome hardship in this way. Of course the matter was different since the doctor, as your grace knows, was deprived of the blessing of sight. But that didn't prevent the Dean of Arabic Literature from donning the turban and jubba and enrolling in that noble university, al-Azhar. As for me, I finished my religious studies in the High Institute of Arabic Music. I was first in the graduating class of 1936 and to this very day I have in my pocket a picture of myself being awarded my degree by His Royal Highness, the King himself." He took out an old page taken from *Photographer* magazine and spread it out between himself and Sheikh Genid, making the other hold part of it. He said, "Look. Here's the King standing there. And here I am, wearing a fez, looking happy and shaking with him—with my right hand." Sheikh Hosni folded the picture up once again and put it back in his vest pocket. "I worked as a music teacher and still do, even though I've never made a single millième's profit from it because the expenses and responsibilities are so great. I'm the one who trained all the composers and musicians you've heard of. You know, the old songs by Abd al-Wahab and *Spring* and *First Whisper* by Farid al-Atrash." Sheikh Hosni came to a halt at the edge of the riverbank and said, "Good evening Zein, my boy!"

Zein the boatman returned his greeting from beneath the dense leaves of the castor palm, "Welcome, maestro!"

Sheikh Hosni turned to Sheikh Genid and asked him what he thought about renting a felucca. But before the other could reply, Sheikh Hosni had taken him by the arm, saying, "Good idea, Zein, my boy!"

Zein heard the words and climbed the stone steps, all the while fixing his scarf around his neck and ears. Embarrassed, Zein whispered in the sheikh's ear, "Quit it! Really, Sheikh Hosni!"

Sheikh Hosni stood on his toes and whispered in Sheikh Genid's ear that "the boy" was afraid due to Sheikh Genid's condition. He said it indiscreetly, then turned to Zein and told him, in a loud voice, that he understood why he was afraid, but there was no reason to continue the discussion. He told Zein not to worry, the two of them would stay close to shore and wouldn't go into the deeper parts of the river. Tapping his shoulder, Sheikh Hosni signaled to Zein and pushed him down toward the boat. He dragged Sheikh Genid behind him and told Zein that the Sheikh was a honored guest in Imbaba and it wouldn't be right to deny him such a request. Sheikh Genid would be generous with Zein and pay him whatever he wished. Sheikh Hosni insisted that Zein himself seat the two of them in the boat so that the guest would feel more secure. Zein the boatman put them aboard, and the two sheikhs sat face to face. Sheikh Hosni said, "My God! It's been such a long time since I've been for a boat ride."

Sheikh Genid gathered his neat jubba around his closed legs. Smiling happily and feeling the warmth from the water's surface, he said, "Truly, the greatest blessings are the ones that God chooses for us."

Fatma

Fatma emerged from Qatr al-Nada Street, strolling leisurely toward Fadlallah Osman Street. The ends of her silk wrap were gathered under her right arm, and her exposed hand swung back and forth. Her slow, confident movements jangled the gold bangles on her arm. In front of the shop, she let her wrap slip from her head, exposing her thick hair. She smiled at the two men there. From behind, the fullness of her right thigh called out from under the long black shawl.

"God crush the mighty!"

That's what Faruq said while following her with his eyes. He threw away the butt of the cigarette that Yusif al-Naggar had given him. He went home, leaving Gaber the grocer alone to look out onto Fadlallah Osman Street from the entrance to his shop.

His mother was completely enveloped by the smoke of the fish on the grill. She sat in the roofless enclosure created by the back walls of the adjoining old houses. As he entered his room Faruq said, "God have mercy on his soul."

He closed the door behind him and lay down on the sofa. But since he wasn't able to fall asleep, he got up, lit a cigarette and then left his room to sit by his mother. She buried the fish in dry bran and then arranged them in the cooking pan on the stove. After the layer of breading turned crispy, burning slightly, she'd flip it to cook the other side then grab the whole fish by its tail and slap it into a plate of sauce seasoned with lemon and garlic to let it cool while she arranged another pile on the grill. Then, snatching them from the water, she gently tossed them on an upside-down pot cover. As Faruq finished his cigarette, his friend Shawqi arrived and said that he'd been looking for him all over the riverbank. Faruq told his mother to stop cooking the fish for a moment and make them some tea. He grabbed Shawqi and the two went back to his room.

Shawqi asked Faruq if he'd heard anything about the memorial service for Amm Migahid, "God have mercy on his soul." When Faruq answered that he hadn't heard a thing, Shawqi said, crossing his legs, that they were going to make a big night out of it in Kit Kat Square and that everyone in the café was asking about Faruq, hoping to have him get them a loudspeaker system from Khalil.

Faruq said, "OK. But why me?"

"Well, I told them that since Khalil is a relative of yours, he might give you a deal on renting the loudspeaker."

"Oh, I get it. You mean I go out and collect the money and then don't show up?"

"Sounds good. Just don't worry about what happens after."

"Are you serious?"

"Would I joke about such a thing?"

"And what about getting the sound system for everybody?"

"Why do you care?"

"Why do I care? Shouldn't I at least understand what kind of trick I'm playing and who I'm playing it on?"

"You don't need to know that right now. What do you need to understand?"

"I just want to understand our scheme."

"No. You just need to get the loudspeaker system. Understood?"

"OK."

"What is it that you need to do right now?"

Faruq said, "I just need to get the loudspeaker."

"The system is all ready to go. Now what else do you need?"

"Where is it?"

"At Khalil's."

"And then, afterwards . . ."

"Afterwards, I'll take care of everything."

"Will you deal with Khalil?"

"Yes, I'll take care of that shithead."

When Faruq asked him who was going to put up the money, Shawqi answered that everybody in the neighborhood would be contributing to the fund. Then he said, "My God, man! You really are a complete idiot."

Shawqi told Faruq to put his clothes on and yelled out to Faruq's mother to hurry up with their tea.

Faruq's mother was in the habit of entering his room, looking at his bare legs and the blanket that would have fallen from the sofa to the floor. Then she'd scream at him to get out of bed and go look for a job. She had this fixed idea that the best time to look for work was at 5 a.m., or even earlier, and that whoever went out the earliest would have the best luck. When Faruq told her that he wouldn't be able to find a decent job since he hadn't completed his army service, she said that he would have to do just like the rest of his family did: go out and get any job he could find. She continued her early morning wake up calls until he started to get out of bed on his own and put on his clothes. He'd leave their street and head toward Shawqi's house. Then he called out in a sing-song voice, "Shawqi, Shawqi . . ." until Shawqi woke up, put on his clothes, and went with him to look for work.

At the beginning, Shawqi tried to get rid of Faruq in all sorts of ways. He came out in his gallabiya and asked why Faruq was making such a racket at that time of day. Then, ignoring Faruq's explanations, he'd leave him and go back inside to continue his sleep. But then Faruq would start calling out again in his melodious voice, "Shawqi, Shawqi. . . ." After that, Shawqi had to resort to tricks. Late one night, when Shawqi was walking Faruq home from Gaber's shop because Faruq was afraid of the dogs, Shawqi said goodbye and smiled deviously at Faruq. He went home and filled up a can with filthy water, pissing in it for good measure. Then he opened the latch to leave the shutters looking like they were closed and sat there waiting. When Faruq came the next morning, Shawqi let him call out for a while. Then, standing on the sofa, Shawqi put his strong hands on the shutters and shoved them outwards. The shutters hit Faruq square on the head, knocking him on his back. At that moment, Shawqi lifted up the can of toilet water and poured it on Faruq. He slammed the window shut saying, "I should kill you too, you son of a bitch!" He pulled the covers over his head and turned toward the wall, smug with how successful his plan had been. But no sooner had he fallen asleep than he was woken up again by Faruq's sing-song voice, "Shawqi, Shawqi. . . ."

Shawqi remained in his place. He carefully lifted the cover and turned onto his stomach. He lifted himself up, leaning on his hands, so that the sofa wouldn't make any noise. He brought his eye up to the shutter opening, all the while hiding his body, but he wasn't able to make out Faruq until he started calling out again. He was there in the lower right corner. By the time he put his hand on the shutter latch to open it, Faruq had disappeared.

When they met that evening at Gaber's, Shawqi said, "You want to keep doing this? OK." He swore on his mother's life that he'd let Faruq sit outside, barking like a dog, from then on, "Until the whole street starts to laugh at you." The next day, Shawqi sat heedlessly, letting Faruq call out. But Faruq continued to cry, "Shawqi, Shawqi" until the noon prayers at which point Shawqi pulled off his gallabiya, threw on a T-shirt and long-johns and went out to murder Faruq. But Faruq, laughing, got away from him near the river. The next time Faruq saw Shawqi's mother, she was buying cheese at Gaber's. He told her that he'd been passing by to take Shawqi with him to look for a job everyday, but that Shawqi had stopped coming. He asked her if she'd heard him calling out trying to get Shawqi to come with him. She said she had been hearing him calling out, but that she didn't realize that it was to drag Shawqi with him to look for work. The next day, when Faruq began his call, he heard a huge argument behind the closed shutters. A few moments later, Shawqi emerged fully dressed. There he saw Faruq gleefully beaming, and he glared at him angrily. Finally, Shawqi began to smile in reply.

They started to leave the house at exactly six each morning. They'd meet up with some of their friends who worked at the Public Printing Press and walk with them until they reached Kit Kat Square. By the time the group reached the bus station, they'd turn their heads, sensing that Shawqi had disappeared. After they'd noticed Shawqi's trick, they'd try to catch him at it, but he'd vanish all the same. And each time, Faruq would make up an excuse, saying that he needed to see "where that son of a bitch had gone off to." Faruq would head toward the Nasser Sporting Club on the opposite side of the square. He'd go urinate in the public toilets that were located next to the outside wall of the Club, then return, passing by Hosna, the newspaper seller, taking copies of *al-Ahram*, *al-Akhbar*, *al-Gumhuriya* and all the weekly magazines he could find. Then he'd go to Awadullah's café where he'd join up with Shawqi who would have already ordered two cups of tea and who'd be sitting there waiting for him to arrive with the papers. At such an early hour, Maallim Atiya himself would be the one serving them. They'd sit there until noon when they'd begin to feel hungry. Then they'd return the newspapers and magazines to Hosna and part, agreeing to meet again later at night. Shawqi would tell his mother that they were still in the training process and that their real work would start the next day. Since that was the case, he wanted to eat immediately and go to sleep so that he could rise early the next morning. As for Faruq, he'd go back to his ground floor room in his family's home. His mother would have gone upstairs to visit his sister whose husband had died in the war. They'd sit in the sun and entertain the kids. Faruq would get his fishing pole from behind the door and go off to the river.

Faruq's mother had finished grilling the fish and making the tea. When she came in the room, Faruq told her that they were gathering donations for Amm Migahid's memorial service. When he asked her for ten pounds, which would cover the family's contribution, she said, "Go screw yourself!"

Faruq said while drinking his tea, "My God, you're a real tightass, woman!"

He put on his clothes and worked out the details of the loudspeaker scheme with Shawqi. They lit a couple of cigarettes and went out the door.

As they were leaving, Fatma emerged from the building next door. She was wearing light green shadow on her eyes, and her lashes were dark with black kohl. She wore a black velvet shawl with braided silk embroidery over her shoulders. The shawl parted at where her small breasts lay hidden under her long-sleeved, collared wool blouse.

She smiled at the two of them and walked in front along the alley of Amir al-Giyush until Fadlallah Osman Street. Once again, Faruq could see the fullness of her bare legs and the mature cheeks under that tight brown skirt. He did not fail to notice the suede of her shoes, the tall, stiletto heels, and the fake fur ankle straps.

Chapter
Six

WHEN HE SAW that Maallim Ramadan had left the café, Usta Qadri English relaxed and sat down. He continued watching from afar until Sheikh Hosni emerged accompanying another blind man.

Qadri's wife, Umm Abduh, had told him that Sheikh Hosni had come around to ask about him more than once. The sheikh had been saying that they hadn't seen him at the café, prompting her to ask, "So, tell me. Where is it you go to when you leave here everyday?"

Turning away from her, Usta Qadri informed her that he went to the café everyday, but since Sheikh Hosni was blind, he of course never saw him. Qadri was a tortured soul and Sheikh Hosni's queries only served to agitate him. He was afraid; he was convinced that all his dirty laundry was about to be revealed to his friends. In spite of this, he found himself driven to hover around the café, though at a distance. Lately, he was spending his nights spying from behind the mosque, watching the patrons come and go, but never finding the nerve to go over there.

The truth is that Usta Qadri wasn't a silly or small-minded person. On the contrary, he'd been proud of himself his entire life and was quite conscious of his lofty standing, that he was different from all the rest. And who were they anyway? Sheikh Hosni? Maallim Ramadan, that jokey fitir maker? Usta Sayyid Tilib, that laughingstock? Qasim Effendi who sat around day and night waiting for a pair of glasses to fix? Sgt. Abd al-Hamid who perched himself on the sidewalk selling cigarettes one by one? All of them were savages and sons of bitches.

In contrast to them, the Usta had worked with the English in the Marconi Company and everybody knew that he had absorbed their refined disposition and manners. But in spite of that foreign influence, he maintained his own sense of style which revealed itself most in his choice of footwear (broad, open-toed sandals) and the way he wrapped his folded scarf around his lean brown neck. He also happened to be very fond of dogs and was often seen feeding them near the café. The dogs knew him well, and he could always be seen with them around him.

Usta Qadri spoke English just like an Englishman. His bosses, who were English, encouraged him in this. Mr. Macmillan, the company director, gave him an old copy of Shakespeare's collected works. He'd grown so addicted to reading it that he'd go around reciting lines by heart while he rode his bicycle, delivering telegrams here and there, until his fame had spread far and wide among clients and traffic police alike.

In the special reception parties thrown for Sir Campbell (or any of the lords that paid a visit to the company) they'd invite Usta Qadri to the club or their houses to drink cognac with them. Then they'd coax him to stand up and, in his deep, warm voice, recite bits of *King Lear* or *Macbeth* or Hamlet's monologue. In their annual parties, they honored him by having him play the part of Othello, under the auspices of the English director, alongside an English Desdemona and Emilia. Usta Qadri was especially enthralled by the speech that began with the words, "Her father loved me, oft invited me . . ." or "Who can control his fate? 'Tis not so now . . ." or "Why, stay and hear me speak. . . ." Likewise, he was infatuated with Miss Margaret, or Maggie, the daughter of the company accountant, who'd play the role of Desdemona opposite him. He'd think about what might happen if he were to marry her. Year after year, he looked forward to putting his hands around her beautiful neck and strangling her. And in her blue eyes, he'd see real love as she fell onto the bed, begging him to spare her, moaning, and then dying. He'd won the respect of his colleagues and surpassed them in getting bonuses and raises until his salary had grown quite large and he had become famous. If it weren't for that, he wouldn't have owned the building that he lived in now. Granted it was old and the income it brought was low, but along with the salary he earned as the temporary overseer of the shift books in the factory of the Cairo Metal Tools Company, it allowed him to live comfortably. His daughter was married and had given birth to a little Qadri. His son Abduh was in the High Institute of Commerce in Zamalek. A feeling of satisfaction flooded over him suddenly: he was known as Usta Qadri English, and he fully deserved to have been born to different parents and raised in a different neighborhood.

Yet, he had spent much of his life in doubt, not knowing for certain if they called him Usta Qadri English sarcastically or out of respect for his proficiency in English, cleanliness, and good manners. Whenever he reminded himself that Amm Omran knew six languages besides Arabic and Nubian, and that nobody ever referred to him by any place associated with those languages, he tried to forget the issue, thinking that although it didn't matter, he was nevertheless an unfortunate man. When these painful doubts circled his mind, as they often did, he'd take refuge in the words of Othello, "Nor all the drowsy syrups of the world shall ever medicine thee to that sweet sleep." And he'd say to himself, "If it were only yesterday! I have tasted sweet sleep not, nor any sleep, for so many long nights." He honestly couldn't recall when he had last slept.

It all began late one night when his wife, Umm Abduh, expressed her desire to eat brain purchased from Zaghlul, the head meat and parts seller. Usta Qadri was appalled. He looked at her with his little eyes sparkling between his white moustache that was unkempt around the edges of his lean face. He couldn't respond to what she said because he was so aghast that she even knew this disreputable man's name and would pronounce it in front of him, especially since he wasn't friendly with Zaghlul nor with those who interacted with him. He had seen Zaghlul standing behind his cart, with his eyebrows and face hair neatly trimmed by Usta Sayyid Tilib, the barber, badgering the women and girls, winking while calling out, "We've got sweetmeats, yes, we've got lots of sweetmeats!" While this was going on, the riffraff of Imbaba would have gathered behind him in the dark building entrance, smoking hash and drinking beer. This provoked a staggering amount of disgust and hatred in Usta Qadri English, a hatred that was bested only by Sayyid Tilib the barber's hate for Abd al-Khaliq, the undertaker. Despite the fact that he was dumbfounded to hear Umm Abduh pronounce Zaghlul's name while snapping her gum on the side of her big, wide mouth, and despite the fact that his surprise never dissipated, the woman continued to press her question until Usta Qadri feared that she'd go completely berserk and end up wandering to Murad Street herself to buy from Zaghlul, "And then we'd have a real scandal on our hands!" he thought. Despite all this, Usta Qadri would reply, without actually mentioning Zaghlul's name, that his meat was putrid and that nobody knew where he got it from. If that's what she wanted, he'd go himself one of these days to the slaughterhouse, because whoever wanted to eat sanitary cow brains had to buy them from a place like that. The next day when Umm Abduh woke him, she had already borrowed a basket for him to take to the slaughterhouse.

Usta Qadri purchased a large calf's head, put it in the basket and got on the tram. He placed the basket next to his left leg, letting it lean against him slightly. He took one of the calf's ears out of the basket and placed it under his shoe so that the head wouldn't go anywhere. Then he took out his copy of *al-Akhbar* and began to read that the government was going to lower the prices of commodities. A pickpocket noticed that Usta Qadri was engrossed in the paper and, finding the scene inviting, took out his sharpened razor, slowly cutting away the calf's ear. Leaving the ear under the broad, open-toed sandals of Usta Qadri, the thief got off the tram carrying the basket and the head. When the tram arrived at the vegetable market, Usta Qadri folded up his newspaper and bent over to pick up the calf's head and carry it over the Imbaba bridge. However, he found that while he'd kept his foot pressed on the big gray ear, the ear had been carefully severed and the head and basket had disappeared. He caught sight of the edge of the cut dripping with blood and was on the verge of reaching down to pick it up, but stopped himself at the last moment. He regained his composure, got off the tram slowly, and stood silently at the station. When the tram began to move, he looked between the crowds of legs and under the seats passing in front of him and knew that even if he were to catch sight of the head, he would be too embarrassed to yell out "Hey there!" or to jump back onto the train and scamper about trying to wrest it from people's feet. He imagined that he might fall while running around or one of the passengers might tell him to leave the head alone, that it belonged to him, "and then we'd have a real scandal on our hands." However, he didn't see any calf's head. He left and crossed the bridge empty-handed and went home where he announced that he didn't like any of the heads he had seen at the slaughterhouse. When Umm Abduh asked him where the borrowed basket was, he yelled at her, saying that it had been lost. He went upstairs to bed, turned his face to the wall and slept. He woke up still angry and left to go to the café. On his way to the café, he heard Zaghlul's laughing voice saying, "And upon you be peace, God's mercy, and his blessings." His anger rising, Usta Qadri felt compelled to turn around. At that moment, he caught sight of a large calf's head hung from the front of the cart, a bunch of watercress stuck in its mouth. He was positive it had only one ear. Usta Qadri continued on his way, but he didn't make it to the café. His feet carried him away. He felt like he was walking through crowds with his ass exposed; even the dogs that normally followed him turned their heads away. For a number of weeks, he continued to leave his house and go along the Nile until al-Mounira, then return through the workers' projects toward the train station. From Murad Street, he'd sneak through Qatr al-Nada and Fadlallah Osman and return home.

He opened his trunk and took out the old book. How many nights did he hide his book under his overcoat, head toward the police station, sit next to the river and reread Othello under the streetlights while pondering his life? Especially now since he saw himself living that very tragedy. Zaghlul was Cassio, the villain. Umm Abduh was Desdemona. The calf's head became the purloined handkerchief. The ear that'd been cut off was the monogram on the handkerchief. Who had played Iago? He thought for a bit, but couldn't quite remember. In any case, since he himself had seen the head with its one ear, he didn't need anybody to lead him like Othello needed Iago. Iago addressed him saying, "I know not that, but such a handkerchief—I am sure it was your wife's—did I today see Cassio wipe his beard with." What would Iago say now? Usta Qadri revised the line, saying, "I know not this ear, but such a head—I am sure it was yours—Did I today see Zaghlul hang on his cart." Usta Qadri wished that instead of leaving the ear on the floor of the tram, he'd picked it up and brought it with him. Then his doubts would have been laid to rest. But how? He could have bought the head from Zaghlul's cart, and brought it home and matched it up to the ear that'd been cut off. But he hadn't thought to save it. He felt a fire burning in his heart and almost exploded with anger.

Then his rage about his son Abduh's late nights out began to subside. Not a sound was heard from him. When he spoke, he talked in a whisper. The sparkle in his eyes went out and he stopped looking into the eyes of those he met. He stopped asking for food or cups of water. And he noticed that his stomach had become somewhat irregular in its workings. He began to fart profusely and, often while sitting by himself in the toilet, he bit his lower lip and turned on the faucet so that the sound of the water would drown out the noise of his flatulence. Once, while performing his marital duties with Umm Abduh, he noticed that his erection dissipated quickly. With time, his mustache also began to go limp. When he heard that Sheikh Hosni had been coming around, asking about him, he began to change the course of his walks, wandering all over creation before he finally returned to Kit Kat Square, where he stopped at a distance like right now, his eyes peering toward the place. Just then, Usta Qadri ducked his head again because he'd seen Sayyid Tilib, the barber, coming from Murad Street and entering the café.

A Relationship

While Amir Awadullah went off to see what was happening with Maallim Sobhi and Maallim Atiya in the steel storehouse, Yusif al-Naggar remained standing in the café doorway.

He had another half hour to kill before going downtown to meet Fatma. He was going to take her to Magid's apartment, spend some time with her there, and return home. He thought he'd try to talk with Amm Omran about Amm Migahid's death. When Yusif sat down next to him, Amm Omran averted his eyes, gazing off in the distance without turning to look at Yusif nor showing him any signs that he'd seen him. Amm Omran often did that. Yusif knew that if he ignored Amm Omran or got up and left, Amm Omran's anger would grow. Yusif had to proceed with caution, to let their conversation proceed naturally. However, tonight he didn't feel up to it, he didn't have enough time.

In this fashion, their relationship would move in fits and starts, would die and come back to life. During long nights, after the café closed and everyone went home, they'd leave the group and leisurely walk under the trees along the riverbank, until they reached al-Galaa Bridge, or "Badia Bridge," as Amm Omran, in his wool slippers and flannel pajamas under a long coat, persisted in calling it. He had white hair, and he told stories in his soft, deep voice. And he'd link arms with Yusif al-Naggar who, with his dark eyes and his black disheveled hair, wore his wool jacket buttoned-up. They'd cross the bridge and head left at al-Gabaliya Street where the massive, quiet buildings stood on the right, where a few, scattered little light bulbs were hung in the tangled tree branches along the river's edge, and where the light was dim on the dirt of the long, empty sidewalk. They'd wander along this street until they reached Zamalek Bridge, then they turned at the carved, dark gray stone entrance with its old, green iron posts supporting dusty, globe-shaped lamps like so many crowns. They'd cross the bridge, until they had a full view of the river. From there, they would veer right toward Kit Kat Square taking one favorite route in the summer and another in the winter. Long nights and endless stories with no beginnings.

Then, all of a sudden, their relationship would unhinge and their conversations would die. They might run into each other, but it'd be as if neither one had ever seen the other before. Amm Omran watched the domino games, sat silently with the gang, or talked with Usta Qadri English without letting Yusif al-Naggar listen to what he was saying. When the café closed for the night, he'd climb up to 'the tower' and spend the night awake on the high roof, or he'd go spend the rest of the night talking with Amm Migahid, who never slept. As for Yusif al-Naggar, he'd go to sit with Salim Farag Hanafi, Amir Awadullah, and some of the others. But often he came late, bought the early edition of *al-Gumhuriya* newspaper, which was sold at night, and, before going home, sat in the café entrance to read and drink a cup of coffee. Other evenings would go by, and the conversation between Yusif and Amm Omran would somehow return on its own accord. It could be that one happened to agree with an opinion the other expressed. It could be a smile. Or it could be they shared an anger about something. This is how their nightly tours would return, as if they hadn't stopped during the long months in between. It didn't seem like they had actually ceased, but rather that they were continuing something that had been interrupted. And the old stories would be recounted. The same endless stories with no beginnings.

Yusif al-Naggar wasn't afraid that this signaled the beginning of a new dispute, since he knew that the disputes wouldn't take place unless there was a shared desire. Neither one was allowed to break things off unilaterally. Whoever wanted to annul the relationship had to put pressure on the other to consent. That's what Yusif al-Naggar had learned and that's what Amm Omran knew. Now, Yusif wanted to listen to Amm Omran talk about Amm Migahid and hear what he thought about what was going on. Anything would suffice. Yusif asked him if he wanted tea, but Amm Omran shot him a look from the side of his eye and, refusing, shook his head. Yusif looked down and saw the edges of his trousers splattered with mud. As he did so, he noticed Amm Omran turn toward him angrily and then recompose himself. He thought he'd get his shoes shined but Gamal the shoeshiner was watching, crossing his legs under his long gallabiya, and completely absorbed in following the domino game. Suddenly, Maallim Ramadan got up angrily, cursed the domino players and made his exit by kicking the oranges that had fallen from his lap under the seats. They both smiled at what had just happened. Yusif al-Naggar asked Abdullah to bring a cup of tea for Amm Omran and a coffee for himself. Amm Omran told Abdullah not to get him anything and Yusif insisted, "Just so I don't have to drink by myself. . ."

"I just had tea."

"Okay, then have anything else."

Abdullah called out, "One dark coffee with half a sugar. And one fenugreek for your Amm Omran."

Abdullah left them and returned again to Qasim Effendi who was sitting on his chair, his paper open in his hands. Yusif said that he'd been out of sorts since hearing what had happened to Amm Migahid. Amm Omran didn't say anything. Yusif said that when he finished his coffee, he'd have to go downtown because he had an engagement, but it wouldn't take long. Feeling the key in his jacket pocket, Yusif thought of Fatma.

One night, Yusif's mother asked him if he knew the young woman named Fatma who lived next door. When he said that he knew who she was, his mother told him that she was married to a young man with a car and that he'd given her family a large sum of money in order to marry her. His mother went on to say that Fatma still lived in the same house with her mother, Umm Sayyid, and her two sisters. When Fatma's husband came to visit, he'd leave his car in the alleyway and Umm Sayyid would sit there, yelling constantly at the kids who gathered around and played on top of it. Yusif's mother did a great impression of Umm Sayyid yelling at them to get away from her son-in-law's car. Yusif had been sitting on the couch in the living room once, reading and drinking tea while his mother sat on the white sheepskin rug spread out over the kilim—the stove, the teapot, and the cups in front of her—and he had seen the car and heard Umm Sayyid and had to admit that her voice was exactly like how his mother did it. Later, his mother told him that the young man who'd married Fatma had left her and gone back to where he came from. Yusif already knew that. He was quite cognizant of the fact that she was no longer a virgin, that she had become a woman. The next time he saw her, he decided he'd let her talk with him and go off alone with her someplace. But after her brother died, he stopped thinking about it and was happy just to return her smile whenever they crossed paths.

Then Fatma started to come over so that Yusif could write letters to her husband for her. The first time, she asked him about the books on his walls. He was fiddling with the desk drawers when he answered her. She nodded her head, looked at herself in the heavy mirror, winked at him and left. The second time, she asked him what the picture hanging next to the window symbolized, and then started to ask him about his books again. She wanted to know if he bought books because they were related to his job, or if he bought books because he read for pleasure. When he told her that he bought them because he liked to read, a look of happiness spread over her face. Resting her thin house dress and her small breasts on the pile of books on the edge of the desk, she asked him in a whisper, "So that means you're an enthusiast?" Yusif al-Naggar smiled and she went back to interrogating him, asking if he ever went to the cinema. He answered that he seldom saw films, that the movies he watched at the local cinema club were enough for him. She whispered, "Suppose someone were to offer you two tickets to the cinema, one for you and one for a friend, or a girlfriend, would you accept them, or would you embarrass that someone by turning down her gift?"

When he said there was no reason to beat about the bush, she said, "Okay, then we'll make it Thursday, since that's your day off."

And with that she left him.

Yusif was reading the next time she came the next time on the pretext of needing to borrow an envelope. She stood in front of him and put her gold-braceleted hand into the pocket of her house dress and brought out the edge of two folded tickets. When she asked him how they were going to meet, he replied, "Didn't you say that these would be for me and a friend of mine?"

She laughed with him and, hiding the tickets, said, "That's right. So, is this friend of yours better than me?"

His right hand let go of the book and told her that he had an appointment downtown on Thursday. He suggested that she give him one of the tickets now, and then they could meet at the cinema when he was finished with his engagement. The tickets were assigned sequentially and that she'd find him in the seat next to her. She said that she already knew that the tickets were numbered. After hesitating for a moment, she gave in and said, "All right."

After Fatma left, his mother yelled that his tea was ready. He went out to the living room, drank the tea, put on his street clothes, and went out to the café. He sat down with Magid and told him what Fatma had been up to, saying that now he didn't know what to do. He even asked Magid to go in his place. Even though she was young, she seemed loose. He went on about her family and her morals, saying that he didn't know what she wanted from him. Magid said that it'd be an interesting experience, especially since she was a local girl, and because this kind of adventure wasn't usually available to local boys like them—and Yusif could dump her whenever he wanted. He promised to give Yusif the key to his apartment whenever he asked. Yusif went on the date, and they met outside the cinema. He was looking for her when, from behind, she wrapped her fingertips around his elbow. The two went up to the balcony, she nestled up to him and he told her that he hadn't seen an Arabic film in at least ten years. Even though he was staring at the screen, she asked him to enjoy himself and pretend there was nobody else. When the film's heroine took off her clothes and turned around, they could see a small mark on her naked back. Fatma leaned her shoulder over to his and whispered, "What do you suppose that mark is about?"

She looked at him from the corners of her almond eyes and he smiled. She pressed into him even more and, looking down into her lap, said, "This skirt is much too short! Don't you think it would've been better if I'd worn pants? At least they'd've kept me warm!"

He looked down and saw her legs, exposed to the thigh, and said to her, "But it's so much nicer like this."

Repressing a laugh, she grimaced and announced that she had a particular medical condition, "I swear, would you believe, when I went to the doctor he said I was suffering because of my separation from my husband. Isn't that amazing?"

Yusif al-Naggar nodded in agreement, but what she'd said stunned him. A little before the film ended, she whispered to him that they should leave. On their way home, she put her hand in his. He told her that he had a friend who'd promised to give him the key to his apartment so that the two of them could get away from the noise of the crowds and really converse. They rode a taxi to Kit Kat Square and got out. He asked her to go on ahead since he was going to pass by the café and didn't want anyone to see them together. She lowered her head and a smile spread across her face.

The following Thursday, she told him about a locked room on the ground floor of her building where they could meet.

Sulayman Jr. got up to search under the seats for the oranges which had fallen from Maallim Ramadan's lap. When he'd found them all, he placed them on top of the refrigerator. He drank a cup of water and then returned to where he'd been sitting.

Chapter
Seven

FROM HIS PLACE on the river's edge, Amir Awadullah could see, beyond the road filled with cars and people, the large sign lit by those lamps with the shades that looked like inverted metal fezzes: "The Steel Storage Company" on one side, "Say a Prayer in the Prophet's name!" on the other. He saw the exterior walls painted blue and yellow, the entrance to the office with its glass exterior, the large iron scales, and the rest of the deep doors that exposed coils of steel reinforcement bars. Amir Awadullah turned around and looked out over the river. He took a few steps sideways until his back was directly in front of the closed glass entrance. He leaned his head further to the right and looked from the corner of his eye into the office.

Maallim Atiya sitting on the right had his back toward Amir. On the other side, Maallim Sobhi's back was also turned toward Amir. Between them, Hagg Khalil's face looked straight at him from behind his desk.

The telephone. The tie. The bald forehead. On the far corner of the desk, he saw the profile of Hagg Hanafi, the large-headed milkman, a wide scarf covering his neck and shoulders, staring at Hagg Khalil's large head. Amir adjusted his position and carefully studied the scene. He couldn't tell who was talking and who was listening. The sidewalk was crowded with little boys spilling out from the garages where they worked: their greasy clothes, their blackened, smudged faces, the sparks of light flying out from their electric welding. Some were taking apart tires and some were lying on their backs under parked cars. The smallest of them had climbed the fender of a truck and was sitting on it, holding a floodlamp to illuminate the motor for the boss, who was half hidden under the hood. Amir Awadullah found all this absurd; he'd come to see what was going to happen with the café. It was as if he'd come to sit with them, even though he had nothing to say. To do nothing but watch from outside. He realized that it was useless to stand there, that he wouldn't learn anything by it. But one thing was certain: this meeting between the maallims would lead to their final agreement. And the final agreement could only mean the café would be lost because Maallim Sobhi was now the café's legal owner. The Maallim's business had grown considerably. He was on his way to becoming an equal to Hagg Khalil himself. Amir said that Maalim Sobhi was creeping and spreading like a cancer through the neighborhood. He'd buy old houses in order to demolish them. As for Hagg Khalil, he was much bigger than all of the maallims put together, running his errands in Imbaba in a Mercedes like some nouveau riche. Maallim Atiya was a small time maallim, and his limits were known to all. On the large piece of land he bought near Mounira, on a foundation that could have supported a ten-story building, he'd built only two floors with four apartments! He was also preparing the new café under the building on al-Wihda Street. But what was Atiya going to gain by this? He'd lose all the old customers, and even if he got new ones, in the end he would just finish the construction of the building. As for Hagg Khalil and Maallim

Sobhi, God only knew what they were after. Certainly, after the knife incident, Maallim Atiya would leave the café. The money he'd taken these past months was more than enough. Amir retreated and sat on the short stone wall on the river's shore. He lit a cigarette and said, "God damn you, Sheikh Hosni."

Some Repercussions from the Boat Ride

Sheikh Hosni felt for the edge of the boat, bared his arm, leaned over a bit, and began to play with the water. As he splashed about, he announced, "Sheikh Genid, the water's really cold!"

Happily, he dried his hand and lit a cigarette. He thought to himself, what form of transportation hadn't he mastered? He had ridden a bike. He had driven a motorcycle. And now, in a felucca rented at Sheikh Genid's expense, he was gliding across the surface of the water. He remembered the day he had rented a bike from Abd al-Nabi, leaving his skullcap as a deposit. He rode the bike down al-Bahr Street, then turned left at al-Garaj Street which had an incline. He stopped the bike and parked it in the doorway to the house of his friend Husayn Abd al-Shafi. He climbed the stairs and knocked on the door, greeting his mother, brothers, and sisters. Then, declining their offer to drink tea with them, he announced that he had to leave. When Husayn asked him why he was in such a hurry, Sheikh Hosni said that he'd left the bike in the doorway and that he wanted to return it to the bike man. Everyone in the house, not to mention the entire street, gathered to see the blind Sheikh Hosni, son of Hagg Muhammad Musa. He'd come all the way from Kit Kat on a bicycle, and they wanted to see how he was going to return on it. In his mind, Sheikh Hosni recalled how he'd taken the bicycle out of the doorway, pointed it in the return direction, and, running with it for a bit, jumped on. He shot out of al-Garaj Street to the surprise of the neighborhood's inhabitants who stood there petrified, talking about what they'd just witnessed, not noticing that the Sheikh forgot to make the right-hand turn from al-Garaj Street onto al-

Bahr Street in order to reach Kit Kat. Instead, his speedy ride continued across al-Bahr Street's width to the riverbank, where he was propelled, still clinging to the bicycle, right into the river.

Sheikh Hosni smiled to himself when he remembered how he was still clutching the handlebars while sunk up to his waist in the water, and how he called out for help to passersby. And because the sun had set, it so happened that people thought he was the river demon that emerged each day to take one or two of Imbaba's children. It didn't take long before a crowd came scrambling over al-Bahr Street to throw rocks at the demon in the water. His voice became hoarse from bellowing, and he felt paralyzed when the clods began to hit the water around him, splashing water and drenching his shaved head. The tears began to pour from his empty eye sockets until his large ears recognized Sgt. Abd al-Hamid's voice from among the many voices shouting along the river's edge. "Hey Sergeant! Hey Abd al-Hamid!" Sgt. Abd al-Hamid heard the voice and demanded, "Who's that?"

"It's Sheikh Hosni!"

"Sheikh Hosni who?"

"Listen. It's me, Sheikh Hosni!"

"What are you doing in the river?"

"Nothing. I was riding a bicycle and fell in."

"A bicycle? You say you were riding a bicycle?"

"I swear to God! Listen to this!"

He rang the bicycle's bell so that they'd believe him.

Sheikh Hosni smiled again when he remembered how he heard Hagg Mahmud al-Shami urging Sgt. Abd al-Hamid to leave immediately, saying, "Amm, we should get out of here right now. I beg you."

And he shouted, "Come on, it's me, Sheikh Hosni, Amm Hagg! Just ask your son Ramadan and he'll tell you! Sheikh Hosni, son of Hagg Muhammad Musa."

At that point, they lit a fire with some paper and saw that it really was Sheikh Hosni, up to his waist in the water, his hands clutching the bicycle.

As for the motorcycle, he didn't ride that until he'd become a full adult. He'd rented it and had Husayn Abd al-Shafi ride behind him to do his seeing. He kickstarted the bike by himself and, pulling in the clutch, put it in first, accelerated, and went flying out along Murad Street, honking the horn to let people know he was coming. People ran from him in every direction. He didn't stop until he rode the motorcycle through the front of the Imbaba Pharmacy, breaking everything in his path, finally hitting Dr. Abd al-Tawwab who was sitting drinking tea behind a curtain that marked off his office. The sheikh knocked the doctor to the right, while he and the motorcycle went down to the left. Husayn Abd al-Shafi, who'd jumped off at the entrance to the pharmacy, caught up to him.

Carried away by his reveries, Sheikh Hosni suddenly blurted out, "May you rest in peace, Husayn."

"Husayn who?" Sheikh Genid asked, puzzled.

"Husayn Abd al-Shafi."

"Who?"

"What, don't you know him?"

Embarrassed, Sheikh Genid answered, "Sorry—I wasn't paying attention, Sheikh Hosni."

"Listen, who in the world doesn't know who Husayn Abd al-Shafi is? Egypt's captain!"

"Really?"

"Of course. The captain of the Egyptian national football team that went to the Munich Olympics in 1936."

"Is he the one we met at the café yesterday?"

"What café? He's been dead a long time. They found him drowned."

Clutching the edge of the felucca, Sheikh Genid asked, "Oh my God. Drowned? How?"

Sheikh Hosni said that he'd drowned the way anyone drowned. Then he added that he didn't actually 'drown,' but committed suicide, since Husayn Abd al-Shafi was an expert swimmer, "You've got to realize that everybody in Imbaba knows how to swim."

"You mean he drowned himself?"

"Uh-huh."

Sheikh Hosni said that Husayn remained on the coroner's table for a long time until they translated the magazine article and figured out his name. "You see, Husayn never carried any identification or money or anything like I do. But he always had with him a page from a German magazine with his picture on it. It was an image of him greeting Hitler at the inauguration of the games. Husayn standing there wearing his football outfit, Hitler standing there wearing his official uniform, a gold crop under his left arm, shaking Husayn's hand with his right. The seats behind them were packed with Germans."

He leaned his body a little to rock the boat slightly and Sheikh Genid said, "That's enough. We seem to have sailed out pretty far."

"Not at all. There's the shore, right there. Next time, God willing, we'll take you from here to the Barrages. But really, I'm amazed. How is it you never heard of Husayn Abd al-Shafi?"

Husayn had the best sense of humor in the world. When Husayn's father died, Husayn didn't own a thing. Nothing. And he was confused about what to do. Since he was the internationally known captain of the football team, he didn't want to create a scandal by borrowing money in order to bury his father. For that reason, he brought out a clean change of his uniform, and took his father down to the river. He undressed the corpse himself and submerged his father's body three times under the pure water. He recited the shahada twice. Then he dressed him in the clean uniform and brought him back to the riverbank. He put his body in front of him on the bicycle, balancing him between his hands, as if he wasn't dead. He took him from here until he got to Sidi Omar and buried him there with Abd al-Khaliq the Undertaker's full knowledge.

Sheikh Genid was listening to this story, sitting still, with his white face and big, blondish beard. His face turned to stone as a deep shock set in. Sheikh Hosni didn't see it, but he could feel it. He happily related the story of how Husayn, at the end of his life, was living in a room on Hawa Alley: a big room with a large crack running the length of one wall. A veritable chasm! When Husayn sat in the room, he could look out and see the sky through the crack, "Just as you and I are able to see it right now." One day he was sitting alone in his room when all of a sudden there was an earthquake that shook the room violently. When the dust settled, the crack had disappeared. At which point Husayn lifted his hands to the sky and said, "Send me one more earthquake, Lord, and give this room a fresh coat of paint!"

The two sheikhs burst out laughing. When Sheikh Genid asked God to bless Hosni, Sheikh Hosni stopped laughing and remembered that he was carrying in his interior pocket a page from a magazine with his picture on it shaking the hand of His Royal Highness the King, back when he had ranked first in his class. He wasn't carrying anything but that picture . . . exactly like Husayn Abd al-Shafi when they found him. The strange coincidence made him nervous, and he said in a soft voice, "Hello there, Zein, my boy."

But there was no answer from Zein.

He said a little louder, "What do you say, Zein?"

But Zein still didn't respond. And Sheikh Genid said, "Have we drifted out too far?"

Sheikh Hosni replied, "The bank's in front of us, right there. I just saw that Zein was asleep and wanted to wake him up."

And he shouted, "Zein!"

But as before, Zein didn't respond.

Sheikh Hosni rolled up his sleeves and leaned over. Slowly, he put his cane into the water to test the depth. When it didn't touch bottom, he took it out. He stretched his other hand toward the oar rests, then drew it back. It began to dawn on him that his fate was sealed: he was going to drown and like Husayn Abd al-Shafi they'd identify his body by the picture from the magazine. He was completely still, for a moment, then suddenly screamed, "Help! We're drowning!"

Sheikh Genid leapt to his feet, his innocent face now pale. He jumped out of the boat, drawing his jubba around him, and disappeared in the river's waters.

Chapter
Eight

IN THE CROWDED bus, Yusif al-Naggar was forced to stand behind the driver's seat. When it approached the Omar al-Khayyam stop, a young woman got up and grabbed the metal pole planted between the stair and the high, metal roof. The man standing on his left approached, grabbing the same pole. The distance between his large brown hand and her small white hand wasn't more than an inch or two. Before the bus came to a stop, Yusif al-Naggar looked and saw the brown fingers gradually relaxing, the big hand slowly sliding down, then clasping the thumb of the small hand. Yusif sensed the hand as it retreated downward in hesitation. He saw the hand hold its position, the white face leaning confusedly toward the hard brown face, and the quick, pregnant glance. When the bus stopped and the doors opened, the wind rushed in and Yusif felt a chill. The two whose hands he'd been watching got off. There was a group of people standing on the stop's wet platform. The young woman rushed in front of them. The man went around behind them. As soon as she passed the crowd, she slowed down a bit and he caught up with her. He drew close to her under the trees and walked next to her. The bus took Yusif away from the scene.

To Yusif this girl looked like Fatma. In fact, he'd started to find something of her in every woman. It could be almost anything.

He recalled the locked ground floor room where Fatma, in a choked, almost adolescent voice had said, "I must be because I didn't turn you on." He remembered her starting to dress angrily, but then laughing suddenly, sitting on his knees and wiping the sweat of frustration from his face with a corner of her blouse. When her face drew so near to his, her brown skin seemed to redden in the light of the small candle. Her eyes had grown darker, and moist with what looked like faint tears. He remembered the strange barren clothes rack, the faded picture of the family inside the frame inlaid with mother-of-pearl, the dark, coffee-colored chest of drawers, and the white, oval mirror. And he remembered her hoarse whisper telling him not to let what just happened bother him, "What's the big deal? These things happen." He remembered her swearing that she loved him anyway, telling him that she wasn't able to sleep until she saw the light in his window, until she knew that he'd come home. He saw her standing, her eyes languid like she was about to fall asleep, and heard her say, "Good night." As soon as he left the ground floor apartment and went out into the cold, dark street, he recovered his desire.

He had to sleep with her, even if it was only once.

Once would be enough, then he could leave her.

If he left her before they did it, she might scandalize him.

He got off at Orabi Square and headed to 26th of July Street where he was to meet her next to the Supreme Court stop. He lingered in front of the government bookstore and scanned the covers of the books on display. He sensed a faint echo in the air. He went around the corner and stood on the sidewalk next to the blue steel cages where different types of birds and Siamese cats were kept. He never went by here without looking at the animals, keeping track of which ones were gone and which new ones had replaced them. He gazed at them from the openings in the different levels of the steel mesh. The Siamese cats were on the bottom, their floor spread with clean yellow straw. Above them, there were the little white rabbits that looked like laboratory rats. Further above, were the pairs of large Maltese and Qatawi pigeons on one level and carrier pigeons with their remarkable chests and the thin ruff etched around their throats. Finally, on the very top, there were the tiny pigeons, the size of white doves (which never cease cooing about God's oneness), the kind that are forbidden to kill. At least, that's what he was told by his friend who raised pigeons and understood them.

Yusif became more aware of the echoing sound, as if a distant uproar were stirring. Was this possible? Yusif thought not. In order to cross 26th of July, he walked through an opening in the guardrail. He saw Fatma standing next to the bus stop. When he reached Talaat Harb Street, the echoes began to resonate against the walls of the massive buildings. He stood at the end of the street and could see that it was blocked off in the distance. Yes. January. It was a demonstration. He was about to signal for Fatma to come over and look, but the crowds who'd heard the noise had grown and pushed them apart. He remained standing in his place until the first wave of demonstrators approached. At that moment, he retreated into the doorway of the government bookstore and stood in front of it by the iron guardrail, grabbing onto the upper cages of the birds to keep from falling down. There was a small, dark young woman being carried on the crowd's shoulders, her head was wrapped in a sash, and she was leading them in chanting slogans against the regime, against the actress Mimi Shakib, whose prostitution ring had just been exposed, and against the recent price increases. When he could make out her face, he waved to her with his free hand, watching the surging thousands as they broke into two streams. One headed through Orabi Square on its way to Ramsis

Square, the other toward Ataba Square. He bent down, jumped to the ground and began following them. He saw his friend Sami walking with his arms clasped behind his back. Yusif accompanied him until the intersection of 26th of July and Muhammad Farid Streets, then stopped silently in his tracks. He stood listening to the distant slogans and chants, then turned around. He looked in the direction of the bus stop, and it occurred to him that Fatma might still be standing there, but he wasn't certain. He turned right toward Orabi Square until he came to al-Alfi Street. The wooden door to the Regal Bar was shut. He pushed on it, entered, and sat at an empty table. Yusif ordered a bottle of rum and began to drink and smoke.

The Boy and the Light

When Amir Awadullah finished his cigarette, he stepped off the low stone wall. He began to wander away, along the river's edge toward the Imbaba Bridge with its large, iron arches. He crossed the road and walked back along the sidewalk because he wanted to pass in front of the office's entrance and get a closer look at the four maallims still sitting behind the wide plate glass window. As he drew nearer to the garage next door, the young boy who'd been on top of the truck's fender jumped out of nowhere and shined the floodlamp into his face. The bright light reflecting off the glass door into his eyes blinded him. In this way, he walked directly in front of the office but saw nothing at all. He continued walking slowly onwards, blinking his eyes.

The streetlights hadn't come on yet. The branches of the trees appeared thick and dark. In the gathering dusk, Amir Awadullah turned around and watched the flickering fires of the vendors' small, red gas lamps hung above the wood carts that stretched off into the distance along the shore. When he reached the bus station, he saw Yusif al-Naggar standing there and hurried toward him. Yusif apologized, explaining that he had to run since, as he'd already told Amir, he had an engagement downtown. Amir told Yusif to wait a second, asking him to come back early because the fate of 'the café problem' was almost decided. He was going over there to wait for Salim Farag Hanafi, Sayyid Tilib, and some of the other café regulars in order to tell them that from now on, "we're going to have to look for another place to meet." Yusif said he'd do everything possible to get back early and got on the bus, waving good-bye to Amir from where he stood behind the driver's seat. Amir Awadullah nodded his head and remained standing at the stop.

Amir was annoyed, but he told himself that there was no use fretting; he'd just have to get used to life without the café. It was bound to go. If not today, then tomorrow. He was certain of it. He'd have to look at it from the perspective of anybody else in the gang. They weren't interested in the café except as a place to sit. In any case, he'd let them know what was happening in order to see what effect it would have on them. He hoped that Salim Farag Hanafi would be there, since he'd be more concerned about the matter than the others, especially if Amir were to remind Salim about their days in Sheikh Muhammad Qutb's Qur'anic school when the two would go together to and from the school, each one carrying a cloth bag with a writing slate inside. And they'd sit next to his father, Hagg Awadullah, drinking their teas then going off. Yes. Salim wouldn't even have to be reminded: he'd been coming to the café regularly ever since those distant days. His friendship with Awadullah had never been interrupted, neither during their time at Abd al-Hamid Shamsham School, nor at the Imbaba-Ismailia Primary School. He hoped that Salim would be at the café when he got there. He had been disappointed to find no one from the gang to talk to but Yusif al-Naggar.

Even though Yusif was an authentic Imbaban, he somehow seemed like a stranger. Amir Awadullah sat next to the doorway to the café and remembered how Yusif had been a fellow student of theirs in Sheikh Muhammad Qutb's school, Abd al-Hamid Shamsham School, and the Imbaba-Ismailia Primary School. He played with them on the bales of hay thrown out for the racehorses stabled behind Sidi Hasan. He was part of the gang that would climb the tree and spy on the Kit Kat Club. He fished and swam with them in the river. He'd even swum across the river with Hamama. Once they swam all the way to Zamalek, and signaled, naked, at the gang from the other side of the river, and then jumped back in and grabbed onto one of the boats carrying clay pitchers from Upper Egypt, which brought them back to our side. Years passed where he never saw Yusif except by chance. Still, they'd never meet without greeting each other. Then Yusif began coming to the café to sit by himself late at night. Their friendship was renewed by Salim Farag Hanafi who kept up with Yusif. Salim would ask him about the books he loved to read and the pictures he drew and kept at home. Amir Awadullah liked Yusif but felt he wasn't a friend like Salim or the others in the group. Yusif would come and slump in his chair, sitting silently the entire time. He'd look at any old thing without uttering a word. He might spend his whole evening like that. When Amir talked with him, Yusif appeared to be interested. He'd let Amir talk on and on. That is, until Amir would notice that Yusif's eyes weren't really focusing on him. In fact, Yusif wasn't paying any attention to him at all. At that point, Amir would feel self-conscious, not knowing whether to stop or continue rambling on. However, when Yusif spoke, his soft voice would search for its words one by one with anxious deliberation. Then Yusif would suddenly finish talking, in the same way that anybody might finish talking about something. Amir was surprised to see Yusif accompanying Amm Omran, staying up late with him. He was also surprised to see Yusif sitting talking to his friends who weren't from Imbaba. But the thing that really confused Amir was how on some days he'd run into Yusif and ask him where he was going, and Yusif would tell him that he was going home to sleep or that he was late for work. He'd say good-bye, and Amir would see him walk in the opposite direction of the destination he'd just mentioned. Amir thought it strange that when he arrived at the café, he'd find Yusif sitting there with a cup of tea in front of him. He would hardly catch his eye, when Yusif would greet him warmly, as if it'd been a long time since they'd last seen each other. This despite the fact that they'd just been talking minutes earlier.

In the beginning, this behavior was the cause of many discussions and jokes, but with time, it began to seem normal. For this reason, Amir wasn't astonished to see Yusif coming from al-Sudan Street, sitting in the café, or sitting behind Khawaga's kiosk drinking beer, even though he'd supposedly just taken a bus downtown. Amir thought that Yusif was nice; he felt a great love for him and really did enjoy running into him. Only last night Yusif was sitting with him at the café. As Yusif finished a crossword puzzle, he said, "That's weird." Then he explained to Amir that he'd just found out that "Tayyis" was Alexander the Great's lover, "Can you imagine?" Amir smiled a little smile. From his place inside the café, he could see the rear of the large Khalid ibn Walid Mosque, moist yellow with old rain.

Its painted iron fence extended the length of the side street branching off al-Nil Street in front of the café. There was a corroded cement pole at the end of the sidewalk. At its top, another pole extended outward holding the large inverted streetlight. The light, which was always broken, hung high over a wooden cart that appeared to float slightly off the ground. It was warped like a small boat, like his father Hagg Awadullah's shoes, which to this day remained forgotten under the big brass bed. The cart was precariously balanced on a chassis of metal rods settled on two wheels with broken spokes. He noted that the axle was chained to the base of the cement pole so that the cart wouldn't be stolen. From here, Amir Awadullah looked at Sgt. Abd al-Hamid, the cigarette seller, sitting on his seat behind the cart, wearing a wool cap with ear flaps and a brown gallabiya under his government-issue overcoat with dull brass buttons. His legs were tucked under his gallabiya, and he was sitting silently, hands in his lap. Then Amir saw him raise a hand and, stretching fingers that had disappeared in the sleeves of his coat, he adjusted the position of a cigarette pack sitting on the surface of the cart. The sergeant put his hand back where it had been.

Amir stood up. He dragged a chair behind him as he crossed the road and climbed the wide sidewalk. He put the chair next to the back wall of the mosque, behind and to the left of Sgt. Abd al-Hamid, and walked over to him to buy another pack of cigarettes. On the top of the cart, he saw a number of packets of maassil, packages of loose tobacco, rolling papers, and packs of cigarettes, some opened, some unopened. At the front of the cart, the lamp was shielded by a cigarette carton wrapped around the little flame. Amir reached into the pile of little strips of shredded paper placed next to the lamp. He took the lamp and used it to light his cigarette. He went and sat back down in his seat. From there he began to observe the café.

When Abdullah saw him return, he went out and stood in the open doorway. But Amir didn't say anything to him. Instead, he dragged his chair in the opposite direction. Abdullah's mind relaxed. He knew that Amir had gone off to learn the results of the maallims' meeting with Hagg Khalil, by God. If he had discovered any news, Amir would have told him, or at least given him a meaningful look. They were always sharing information, never hiding anything from each other. Abdullah was an insider at the café and was always up on what was new with Maallim Atiya and whomever he talked to, and he always passed everything on to Amir. Sgt. Abd al-Hamid studied what was going on with Maallim Sobhi's group and told Abdullah who listened and then told everything to Amir. Amir would then dot the i's and cross the t's while explaining everything to him. The news that Sgt. Abd al-Hamid obtained about Maallim Sobhi's networking with the hash dealer Haram was what made Amir put two and two together and figure out that Maallim Sobhi was going to buy the building and the café. Abdullah didn't believe the story at first, since he couldn't see Haram having anything to do with the matter. However, the incidents of the last few days tended to confirm its truth. Abdullah went into the middle of the street and asked him, "You want coffee or tea?"

Amir nodded his head without saying a thing. Abdullah hesitated slightly, then turned around and stood in the doorway to the café. Putting his hand in his apron, he shouted, "A dark tea for Amir and make it a good one!"

Chapter
Nine

MAALLIM RAMADAN ATE the other half of his orange as he watched Usta Sayyid Tilib who'd gone off on Murad Street. He said, "There's no strength or power save in God!" He crossed his legs, though he had to grab one with both hands so it didn't pop out out of place. This was a real possibility since his legs were rather short and chunky and wouldn't stay on each other without being forced. Maallim Ramadan had become a real maallim since he'd stopped selling fitir and basbusa and retired.

In the beginning, everyone was baffled, especially Usta Sayyid Tilib who was astonished when he saw him fire his assistant and sit idly in front of his shop. He had assumed that Maallim Ramadan was cracking up as a result of family problems. Yet, there he was, laughing and joking and taking special care of his appearance by getting a shave each day. Usta Sayyid, the barber, got sick of Maallim Ramadan since he had to remove half the Maallim's whiskers with tweezers. Later, he saw the

Maallim bring his children to remove the glass storefront, so that nothing remained but the oven. "He's gone crazy!" Usta Sayyid said, "The hashish must have gotten to him." Finally, they understood. Maallim Ramadan had been purchasing government subsidized flour and sugar with the store's business license and then selling the stuff on the black market. His family was living well on the profit.

"Really, as long as this generates an income, why should I go back to standing in front of an oven all day?" Maallim Ramadan would say. And he felt sorry for Usta Sayyid, whose business did not prosper like other barbers who had electric hair dryers or shampoo. "That's what he gets for going to mulids," he thought.

Maallim Ramadan remembered the time long ago when Usta Sayyid came with his neatly parted black hair and his starched suit to rent the place that became their hash den. He recalled the spot and the times they'd spent there and Sheikh Hosni and Husayn Abd al-Shafi ("God have mercy on his soul!"). He began to shake with laughter when he remembered the time they went, stoned out of their minds, to dawn prayers during Ramadan. In those days, Sheikh Hosni was the imam of the small mosque down by the water. When they emerged from Hawa Alley, Abd al-Khaliq, the undertaker, looked and saw that Zein was about to perform the call to prayer and he said, "Better catch up, Sheikh Hosni! Zein is about to call us to prayers, and we haven't had our last sip of the night yet."

Sheikh Hosni yelled out, "Zein boy! Hold off the dawn call to prayer a bit until we finish getting something to drink."

Zein waited for them to cross the street and drink the cold water from a jug under a tree. Then he began the call.

Maallim Ramadan tried to stop laughing and wash the orange off his hands, but when he remembered the night of the maamur, he couldn't stop. "God, I hope all this laughing is a good sign," he chuckled.

Amm Omran Carries a Late Night Message from the King

Every time that Sgt. Abd al-Hamid went to the spot, he'd bend over, look under the door, and say "hello" until the regulars noticed him. Maallim Ramadan would get up, lift the iron bar and go back to where he was sitting, while the sergeant lifted the door, crouched to enter, and then lowered the door behind him. Before the sergeant sat down, Hagg Morsi would invariably ask him to put the iron bar back in its place. And Usta Sayyid Tilib would tell the sergeant to please take his rifle off and put it far away from the fire.

Sometimes, they left the sergeant out in the cold while they sat inside talking and smoking and pretending not to notice him. Abd al-Hamid tried to get their attention by kneeling down in the street, sticking his rifle under the door, and banging its barrel around, but to no avail. Those inside would roar with laughter and he could be heard laughing out loud too. Then they'd hear the sergeant's footsteps as he walked away some distance, so as not to create a scandal, since the spot was supposedly empty. But soon, he'd hurry back, at which point they let him in, and I'd sit with them for an hour or two. One night, he got up to go out and make sure that everything was all right around the Kit Kat Club. Upon emerging, he turned toward Awadullah's café where he saw the maamur, his assistant in charge of investigative work, and a group of police officers and detectives coming from the opposite direction. Since he was so loaded, he couldn't mumble more than a couple words of warning to his companions, which none of them heard. He ran off toward Qatr al-Nada, his long rifle slung over his shoulder and went to Usta Qadri the English's house, from which he could observe what was happening.

The maamur and his entourage walked up and saw the smoke spilling out from under the spot's door, which was slightly ajar. The officers halted. One of them bent over and saw the companions talking obliviously amid the smoke. As he always did, Maallim Ramadan looked out under the door and, recognizing the black winter uniform with the yellow brass buttons, he assumed that Sgt. Abd al-Hamid had returned. He got up, removed the iron bar and blurted, "So you decided to come back, you jackass!"

He straightened up and saw himself in front of the maamur and his assistant. Maallim Ramadan stood there, his hands over his head, clutching the edge of the door, completely paralyzed. Then he shuddered and said, "What shitty luck. This here is the government, boys!"

Usta Sayyid Tilib, the barber, immediately fainted (afterwards, he said that he passed out because the hashish was of poor quality). But the assistant ordered him to stand and sober up before he got the shit kicked out of him. The officer told them not to move from where they stood. He looked at their hands, under their feet, and searched their pockets. But he didn't find anything because Sheikh Hosni had hidden the hashish in his big mouth (when everyone asked him later where it went, he said he accidentally swallowed it). The maamur then asked them for the whereabouts of the beat cop named Abd al-Hamid. Ordering them to stand in a single-file line, he started walking them under an armed guard. Sgt. Abd al-Hamid saw them walking like this down Murad Street, and he followed from a distance. After that, Maallim Ramadan raised his head and saw his father Hagg Mahmud al-Shami standing on their balcony in his gallabiya and cap. Riveted in his place, he was staring out over the street. That's because everyone knew how angry Hagg Mahmud always was, and how he would still hit his children long after they'd grown up and married, with any piece of metal he could find and in front of everybody. In his violent fits, while raving unintelligibly, it seemed that he really did want to kill them.

So that it would look like he was only a spectator and not a participant in the event, Maallim Ramadan asked the police to let him walk beside, and not in, the line. The officers erupted at him, grabbed him by the throat, and, dragging him by his clothes, began heaping insults upon him. In the end, they didn't succeed in budging him one bit: he seemed to prefer dying right there to passing by his father in that line. So they eventually allowed him to walk alongside. When they passed under the balcony, Maallim Ramadan began to laugh out loud while feeling around in his pockets. Looking up at the balcony, he feigned surprise at seeing his father and greeted him. The Hagg didn't return his greeting, but instead bent over the edge of the balcony and stared at him, the police, and that long, ignominious line walking silently along. Maallim Ramadan hurried away waving his arms in glee until the procession reached Kit Kat Square where the maamur ordered them to stand in a row against the wall, right behind the Royal Winter Hall and next to the door the king had used to enter the famous nightclub. Sgt. Abd al-Hamid said that when he came closer to peek, he saw the maamur make them stand in front of him like schoolboys while he yelled at them saying that it was the first time in all his career to find the respectable merchants of the neighborhood smoking hashish inside a store on Murad Street, the central road of the district! The maamur placed his hand on his waist, paced down the row, and said that it was ludicrous to think that the day would come when he'd see those in whom he'd placed so much trust doing this sort of garbage. Model citizens! The most prominent and distinguished members of the community! Those who should be examples for the innocent children of Imbaba becoming so wanton and licentious! "You dirty scumbags!" Suddenly he asked them about the blind man who had been with them, and one of the officers said that he was pretty sure that Sheikh Hosni had in fact disappeared. Then the maamur said that this would be the last time he'd let them off with just a warning. When it occurred to Sgt. Abd al-Hamid that his name had been repeated once too often, he backpedaled and hid himself. At that moment, the king's door opened, splitting the row of criminals. Amm Omran, the club's cook, peeked out and informed them all that His Highness, the King, was indeed present and had requested that they lower their voices. They were so loud that the king couldn't hear himself speak. The maamur paled and whispered that this would be the last time he'd be so lenient with them and that they should get lost. They hurried away taking long steps until they reached Murad Street. When Maallim Ramadan saw his father still standing on the balcony, he didn't hide himself, but rather stood where his father could see him without hearing what they talked about. However, the Hagg left the balcony and went inside. Sgt. Abd al-Hamid appeared and Hagg Morsi told him, half-crying, that they were going to court martial him, imprison him, and kick him out of the army, since he'd left the king in the Kit Kat Club to come over to smoke hashish instead.

Maallim Ramadan stood on the empty flour sacks behind the oven and washed his hands under the sink faucet. Leaving his shop, he headed toward the café while taking a handkerchief out to dry his hands and wipe his mouth. His father had come back onto the balcony in his cap and gallabiya, but Maallim Ramadan continued going in the direction until he got close to the café. From afar, he saw a large pack of dogs and realized that Usta Qadri must be somewhere in the vicinity. He looked closely and recognized Qadri's brown face and big white mustache peeking out from behind the mosque. He went off to the right and, hiding himself behind Khawaga's kiosk, started peeking himself, squinting his eyes, and swearing he'd bet anything that that was Usta Qadri English. Maallim Ramadan tried to figure out what the Usta was looking at from far away, but he couldn't. Ramadan stepped backwards, then turned and walked to Kit Kat Square. He approached slowly until he was standing directly behind Usta Qadri who was adjusting his crotch, hiding his body, and spying out over the wall. The Maallim put his hand on Usta Qadri's shoulder, startling him, and said, "Lovely evening, isn't it, Usta Qadri?"

He pulled Usta Qadri by the hand over to the café where the gang greeted him like a long lost brother. He shook hands with Qasim Effendi, Usta Sayyid, Amm Omran, and Abd al-Khaliq as if he were being introduced to them for the first time. When Usta Qadri finally sat down, Usta Sayyid leaned toward him and said that they'd sent for him, gone to his house, and asked about him. But his family would always say that he was at the café, "So, what's the story?"

Usta Qadri was greatly relieved and told them that he'd been occupied with his work and that even now he was still very busy. An ambivalent smile appeared on his face, but, since he was unsure about whether they knew about the calf's head, he refrained from saying anything else. He was happy to lean forward, stare at his feet and listen respectfully to Usta Sayyid Tilib's suggestion that they put up a small placard and two dozen chairs in the courtyard for the memorial service. But Abd al-Khaliq, the undertaker, laughed and said that because the weather was so cold, there was no reason to spend all that money. It'd be better if they held the service in one of their own homes, since the whole thing would only take an hour or two, and so long, farewell. Usta Qadri English raised his head and suddenly offered to host the event at his place. As he said this, he felt that something had been reborn in him. He repeated the offer even after they had all agreed, and Abdullah came to take their orders. Rather than going off to fill them, he stood looking at the gang, thinking that they had become complete again. Turning his thin neck toward Qasim Effendi, Abdullah asked him whether or not he'd already told everybody what was in the newspapers. They all stopped what they were doing and turned to Qasim Effendi who looked back at them, with his slight build, small face, and large ears. He uncrossed his right leg from his left and reached into his jacket pocket. Taking the paper out, he opened it to the crime blotter and began reading out loud the story of an Italian named David Mousa who was visiting Egypt and had filed a complaint with the Chief of Police in Imbaba against the citizens of the Kit Kat neighborhood on the grounds that they had illegally appropriated land which was his rightful property. He claimed to have purchased the land in 1944 from a certain Mrs. Nafisa Mustafa Ouda Pasha according to deeds of sale, which were registered at the Egyptian Property Court that same year. And there were other deeds from one 'Khawaga Ferdinand,' representing the Swiss Club in Imbaba, obtained by Mr. Mousa during his residence in Egypt which commenced in 1900 (and during which he obtained Egyptian citizenship, registered in Egyptian schools, and completed his law degree in 1923) and ended when he left the country in 1956. For a moment, Qasim Effendi stopped reading and commented, "No way! What else does this say?" The article added that when Mousa arrived in Egypt on August 19 and went to have a look at his properties, which included the area of Kit Kat and stretched for several blocks, he was surprised to find squatters all over the place and that tall buildings and commercial areas had sprung up on them. But what really astounded him was that the main road cut right through his properties. At this point, the Italian brought forth all the supporting court documents. Qasim Effendi folded his newspaper and returned it to his pocket, saying that while the Public Prosecutor was investigating the matter, you all were sitting around like a bunch of idiots. Maallim Atiya arrived limping slightly. Abdullah noticed the limp when he entered to sit on the chair behind the café's little desk. He looked carefully at the Maallim's rear and saw that his pants were unusually tight, and bulged on one side, perhaps because of wads of bandages underneath. Abdullah turned and, catching the eyes of Sgt. Abd al-Hamid, became certain that the sergeant's story about the knifing had been correct and that the Maallim had actually been wounded below the belt. He nodded and stood in the café doorway, putting his hand in his apron pocket. Right then, he was startled to see the Great Haram come into the café, "Abdullah. One coffee. No sugar."

Abdullah turned around and noticed that Haram had seated himself apart from the gang, next to Sulayman Jr., who was watching Maallim Ramadan telling Faruq to go over to Khalil Ibn al-Disuqi to get the loudspeaker (at a discount) since they were doing this for the memorial. Then Maallim Ramadan asked Faruq if Khalil really was related to him like Shawqi had said. Faruq nodded and asked for four pounds, since that'd be the minimum acceptable amount. When Maallim Ramadan hesitated and said that the total sum they'd collected didn't amount to more than five pounds, Shawqi stood up angrily, threatening to leave. He had thought that Faruq was going to ask the group for a full seven pounds. Qasim Effendi, sitting next to them on the other side, said, "Give him the money, Faruq's a good guy." He gave Faruq a serious look, but Faruq didn't bother to respond. Maallim Ramadan gave him the four pounds, while Usta Sayyid reminded him to try to get as big a discount as possible, since everybody had pitched in and because all the donations would be spent on the event. He told Faruq to explain this to his relative "rationally" and then to go see Sheikh Hamada al-Abiad since the sheikh had agreed to recite prayers for the deceased at Usta Qadri's. Shawqi announced that he was going to accompany Faruq in order to make sure it got done properly.

When Khalil Ibn al-Disuqi saw them standing in the doorway of his furniture shop, he stood up from behind his felt and glass covered desk. Looking them over for a moment, he said, "Welcome, please come in."

Shawqi was moving nervously, mumbling curses about the world and about people who couldn't understand things beyond what they could see directly in front of them. Ibn al-Disuqi took out a pack of cigarettes and forced one on each of them, all the while feeling nervous because he knew the ill-tempered Shawqi all too well—they had served together in the artillery forces. He asked one of his errand boys to bring some tea and repeated again, "Welcome, welcome." Khalil remembered Shawqi arriving late for the morning drills. The drill sergeant grabbed him while he was sneaking through the rows and gave him a hard slap on the back of his neck. Ibn al-Disuqi remembered Shawqi grabbing the front of the sergeant's shirt. Then Shawqi lifted the sergeant off the ground, and, in front of all the soldiers and officers, butted him with his forehead. Blood flowing, Shawqi let him fall to the ground with a concussion. After that, whenever Khalil saw Shawqi, he was in the stockade. Whenever they released him, Shawqi would grab any officer he could get his hands on and head-butt him. Blood would flow until Shawqi would be sent back to the stockade. "Glad to see you," Ibn al-Disuqi said while stirring his tea.

Faruq did all the talking and explained the situation. Since Amm Migahid didn't have any family, everyone had to help out. Despite the fact that Ibn al-Disuqi had been following along with interest, he became distracted, attempting to hide his anxiety. Most of what was said ended up passing him by. When he noticed that Faruq had finished, he reached to take a wallet from the inside pocket of his jacket. But then he thought that it wouldn't seem appropriate and he pulled his hand back empty. He pretended to be busy by putting the empty teacups back on the tray. When he sat down, Faruq said that the guys at the café wanted him to lend them a loudspeaker system so that Sheikh Hamada al-Abiad could read from the Qur'an. Khalil Ibn al-Disuqi looked out of the corner of his eye, noticed the rage boiling in Shawqi and stood up again. He announced that of course he wouldn't make them pay any rental charge but that he couldn't let a loudspeaker go out without a safety deposit. Shawqi, also standing up, replied that if a stranger were to overhear this conversation "He'd say that you didn't trust us. And that's not right, Khalil. You should be ashamed." When he slapped a heavy hand on Khalil's shoulder, he raised a small cloud of dust. Shawqi lowered his hand and spat, "Disgusting! What was that?" And, turning to Faruq, "You! Get your ass up."

Shawqi went over to the metal amplifier case and put it under his arm. Before walking out, he turned around and grabbed the stand. Faruq went over to the large metal speaker and hoisted it on his shoulder with the long electrical cord wrapped in a bundle. He also grabbed the microphone from a shelf in the glass counter filled with assorted teacups and water glasses. The two of them left while Ibn al-Disuqi walked out behind them fuming, telling him that they would be responsible for anything that happened to the amplifier, loudspeaker, microphone, and cord. But they ignored him and headed straight to Usta Qadri's house where they put down their load. Then Faruq took the speaker, some wire, and the cord, crossed the street to Sgt. Abd al-Hamid's house where he climbed up to the tower where Amm Omran lived. He attached the speaker to the wooden pole and pointed it out, toward Kit Kat Square. He threw the cord down to Shawqi who brought it in through the window of Usta Qadri's house. Faruq knocked on Umm Shorbat's door, entered, and stood in front of Umm Ruwayih, the mother-in-law of Sulayman Jr., the goldsmith. Looking at her bared legs as she sat cross-legged on the sofa in front of the television, they asked her if Sheikh Hamada was home. She looked at the two of them with her laughing eyes and said that he was. Then she asked Faruq about his mother, and he told her that he was looking to find her a new husband. They went upstairs, Faruq exchanging looks with Shawqi who was already more embarrassed than he. Sheikh Hamada received them by blocking the door with his body and staring at them with his amazing albino face. He told the two that he had an appointment to recite for some people on Sidi Ismail Island and that when he finished there he'd come right over. Shawqi—who was watching the sheikh's silver eyelashes flashing over his red, pinched eyes—objected. He asked the sheikh to come to Usta Qadri's house first, and then he could go wherever he liked afterwards. Faruq and Shawqi returned and hooked up the stand and microphone. Shawqi asked how much of the money they still had, and Faruq said that it was the whole four pounds. To which Shawqi replied, "You are correct."

Faruq turned on all the switches and began to adjust the volume, saying, "Now for a sound check." He asked Shawqi to speak into the microphone, and Shawqi said, "Halloo. Hallooooooo," then smiled. Faruq grabbed the loud, scratchy microphone, and crooned, "Ladies and gentlemen, boys and girls. This is Voice of the Arabs broadcasting from Imbaba City. Coming to you live from the apartment of Usta Qadri English."

Chapter
Ten

YUSIF AL-NAGGAR BEGAN to feel the effect of the small bottle of rum and asked the bartender to bring him another. He'd completely forgotten about Fatma until he searched in his pockets for a box of matches. His fingers stumbled upon the key to the flat. He thought of her, but the echoes of the chanting demonstrators rang in his mind, softly, ceaselessly. He didn't know what had come over him exactly, or what had made him come to the bar to drink alone. He thought of the young, dark woman he had seen being carried on the crowd's shoulders, her hair wrapped in a scarf, and he was fascinated by her bravery—a bravery he didn't possess—and by the visible anger that had transformed her features. That child-like woman. He remembered Mansour and Fathi and Fayyad and Abd al-Qadir and, counting the years, realized that it'd been five. The night that Abd al-Qadir took you out and you drank with him. But that was in another bar and long ago, and you weren't alone. He ate a handful of soaked ful beans and poured himself a shot, thinking about the novel he wanted to write and the pages he'd filled up with notes. Despite the years that have passed and your present drunkenness, you still remember everything, because you've already written it dozens of times, though you did nothing with the material afterwards. It was raining. That's because you began your novel by talking about the rain, about your leaving the house after having an argument with your father, who was still alive then, and then going to Awadullah's café and then riding the bus and getting off at Orabi Square and then heading to Talaat Harb Square where the first things you saw were the circles of people gathered around a student, and the large crowd where you stood and the fair man with short brown hair debating that student in a calm voice in front of all the people, talking about the state of the country and the occupation of the Sinai which made it necessary for everybody to disperse and go back to their business. This man's eyes, arching wide, full of warnings and threats, were staring intently into those of the student. You've never forgotten that glare. You'd recognize that face in a pile of decapitated heads, but you've never written about it. You believed Abd al-Qadir immediately when he told you that it was people from the secret police who staged such discussions in order to get everybody to think that they alone were the rational citizens taking a stand against anarchy, and to make the students look like a bunch of irresponsible hotheads making some mistake. Abd al-Qadir knew all that without actually looking at the man, and he knew all that without ever leaving his seat at the café, but you, you don't know these things and you're unable to believe in things unless you see them with your own eyes. You didn't write about that, but you did write about how the painted slogans on the walls were still wet. You didn't write about the people who crowded the sidewalks to watch but you did write about others standing behind them, tottering on their toes to watch the mass demonstration and the riot police lined up in front of the Air France office with their night sticks and neat riot shields and your leg that got injured when you collided with the metal garbage can in front of the building while you were trying to get to the café and your friend Mustafa the painter who said that all cops looked exactly alike because they'd been hatched from the same eggs and the traffic lights in Talaat Harb Square whose green, yellow, and red lights would blink on and off at the streets that fed into the square and you found it strange they should do that when there wasn't a single car coming or going. What made you want to write about some details and not others, details which you wouldn't remember now but for the fact that you wrote them down? Then there was the man who argued with the student and stared at him, whom you've always remembered without having written anything about him down. You wrote about some things and not about others. You wrote about how you sat with everybody in the passageway at Café Riche and the small fliers which Fathi wrote out with the ball point pen and how each person took a sheet of paper and folded it over a piece of carbon paper and copied out the written statement and made two copies and then tore the sheets in half and put them on the stack on the table. You wrote about how the others like you sitting in the back of the café were forced to sit cross-legged and copy things using their knees as tables, and each time you stood up and leaned over those who were sitting, you had to stretch out your hand to put the two pieces of paper on top of the other copies . . . . You didn't write about the text of the manifesto but instead about the window overlooking the café and the empty tables and the cotton tablecloths with blue and red embroidered edges, and the big refrigerator whose frosted glass door always prevented you from seeing what was inside, and the packet of paper on top of it, and the long-necked bottles and the flowers and the stairs and the doorway to the toilet and the cold air. And Qasim who purchased five yards of white cloth and a bottle of blue ink and how he told you not to give a copy of the declaration of solidarity to every single person because there weren't enough copies to go around and that instead you were to give one copy to each group, and you telling him that you wanted to go with one of them and Qasim telling you everybody would go in pairs and you taking your share of the fliers and going with them to Tahrir Square where you saw the students who'd taken it over, and the foreigners who stood in front of the Izavitch Café and the cameras and movie advertisements on the huge billboards and the words that had been added to the marquees to change their meanings and scraps of paper everywhere and the ripped up cobblestones blocking the roads and you walking on with Fathi while he distributed his fliers and exchanged funny remarks with the crowds and you distributing your fliers but feeling embarrassed and out of place. You didn't write about that, but you did write about the bodies and clothes and shoes . . . high-heeled shoes, flat shoes, worn-out shoes, shoes that were falling apart and ground down on one side . . . black shoes, yellow shoes, red shoes, shoes with laces, shoes without laces, shoes that covered the entire foot, and boots covering part of the leg . . . and the legs, some moving and some planted, legs packed against one another and legs moving freely, bare legs, legs covered by clothing . . . and the clothing, light clothes, and heavy fabrics, jackets ripped on the back, jackets whose sides were torn, sweaters, blouses colored and with designs, and hands carrying books and papers and bread and handkerchiefs and pens and white faces and brown faces and angry eyes, laughing eyes, staring eyes, and fearful eyes. Short hair and long hair and furious bodies moving to and fro around you. You wrote about how Samir and Farag and Sami bumped into you while they ran, carrying their bags and them asking you for a copy of the flier, which they took and disappeared. You and Fathi reaching the round cement platform and finding that Qasim and Fayyad and Atiya had gotten there before you and written a slogan with blue ink on the white banner and hung it up on the marble monument next to the other banners. The noise had subsided since sunset and you saw everybody from where you were above. They gathered in droves, backs to the monument, the movement at the edges of the square had quieted, and they began to sing "Biladi, biladi" and Fathi, Mansour, and everybody were singing. You wrote about the night and the distant stars and the base of the large stark monument in the heart of the square, and the many banners and the thousands of people moving as if they were a single mythical creature which covered the grass and asphalt and sidewalks, and the singing growing louder and louder like a roar pouring through the wide streets that opened onto the square: al-Bustan, Qasr al-Aini, Sulayman Pasha, Qasr al-Nil, al-Tahrir Street. You wrote about that, but you didn't mention that no matter how much you tried to join in, you couldn't raise your voice and sing and you wondered what was stopping you since no one could hear you or distinguish your voice from the others anyway, and you chanted a line or two from that anthem you love, but something like embarrassment held you back. You wrote about the Republic Theater and the National Theater when you went to meet the actors and actresses and to get their signatures on a petition and, behind the thick backstage curtain you lifted, the famous young actress in her crowded room who invited you in and kissed the woman who was with you, her fingers pushing away a lit cigarette while signing her name on the first line, and everyone with her signing their names beneath hers and the young woman with the velvet pants and green t-shirt whose décolletage appealed to you. You wrote about that, but you didn't write about how your woman friend leaned over and whispered in the ear of the actress that the guy standing next to you was her fiancé and you figured that out when you saw the actress raising her eyebrows and shaking his hand one more time making sure that the two of them would drop by to visit her again. You wrote about that other, out-of-the-way dressing room where you found the older theater actress with her familiar face, her cosmetics table crowded with small implements and the tall mirror and the empty leather couch and the silk dresses sparkling in the corner under the bare electric light bulb, and the long-haired wig when she stood in the middle of the room, the rouge on her cheeks and lips while she read the manifesto, the sleeve of her dress rolled back over her bony wrist and the crying tears which rolled from her eyes and smeared the rouge on her cheeks, and her asking for the pen to sign, her shaking hand, and her saying without drying off her tears how honored she was that we'd asked for her autograph. You had no idea exactly what play was running at the time, but you wrote that it was Hamlet and the old woman was Hamlet's mother, the queen, and that you heard Horatio saying, "Now cracks a noble heart. Goodnight, sweet prince. . . . " And the Writers' Union which they closed in your face with iron chains and the Journalists' Union where you met up with the others and then Abd al-Qadir found you and invited you to come with him to Venicia Bar, and when you two had drunk some, he told you about how society had changed, and how its people, soil, and trees were there to be exploited by whoever was willing and able, and he asked you not to get too depressed about the way things had turned out, and he said that he'd heard an announcement on the radio from some of the actors who'd signed our petition at the Republic and National Theaters who, after realizing the danger of the situation, had changed their minds and were now supporting the government, and he said that student movements never manage to overthrow regimes, but only forced them to change their clothes, when their crotches—usually hidden so well under silk and iron and firepower—began to wear out, exposing their private parts, and he said that lately these regimes had made preparations for such dangers and maintained a supply of these clothes in all sorts of colors and that the real problem emanated from the sort of people on the street who stood watching and pointing fingers of blame, and he said that he'd heard with his own ears people from the underclasses saying that the students were protesting because they were young and had parents who paid for everything and that they really care about anything. When the two of you left the bar, Abd al-Qadir said that the nation was undergoing a profound transformation and that we were the last bastion of the old guard and that the most important thing now was to keep what we'd gained so that the nation would always belong to us and you told him that you weren't able to sing along with everyone and he looked at you and smiled, saying that you'd reached the riverbank, and that now he would go home since the situation wouldn't change before dawn and you asked him why and he told you that the police would attack the square at dawn, beat up and arrest the students, and break up the demonstration because the square had to be empty by the time people get up for work and he told you to trust him and to go home since he was going right then and he stopped a taxi and got in and you feared that the effects of the alcohol on you might still be noticeable, so you sat on the edge of the wide river and you enjoyed the view of the thin obelisk and the minaret, near the ruling party's headquarters, flooded with yellow light in the midst of the night's blackness, and the palm trees leaning in the breeze and you felt cold and rose to cross the street between the Semiramis Hotel and the Shepheards Hotel and you headed toward Qasr al-Dubara Square and the Anglican Church and you saw the large, tarp-covered trucks on the dark street behind the Mugammaa building, the seat of the central bureaucracy. There wasn't a sound except the noise of the officers' feet as they threw packets of food and oranges to the conscripts sitting inside the trucks, and you stayed up all night with Amal and his Kuwaiti friend on the balcony of the Bahri Building overlooking the square, and at dawn the people who still occupied the sloping lawns inside the traffic circle held hands and refused to budge when the government troops approached, hitting them with their clubs and dragging them by their hands and feet and the screams of the girls on the pavement grew louder when the soldiers threw them in the trucks and left. When you said goodbye and went downstairs, you saw a number of men dangling on rope ladders from the tall base of the monument, washing the blood from the walls, and each one was carrying a small bucket and a big, thick paint brush. The banners had disappeared, and in the middle of the square, other men knelt, picking up the rocks and pamphlets from the pavement of the wide streets. When you walked behind the Hilton Hotel to catch the Imbaba bus and saw all the people getting off their buses, you noticed the traces of sleep in their eyes, you wrote about that, although you wrote "Fuck the people with sleep in their eyes, and fuck the theater and the actors and actresses. Goddamn your girlfriend and her fiancé and Mansour and Fayyad and Fathi and Qasim and Abd al-Qadir and goddamn this country and goddamn you all." Yusif ate a handful of soaked ful and thought, "You're drunk. You shouldn't write about them. You should write about the things you know. Write about Amm Omran or Abdullah or the café or your father who died. Write that when a poor person dies, it isn't a death. It's more like an assassination. Better not to write about any of these things. You should write about the river and the stone huts on the banks and say that every house has children who live in it, and you should write about the boys fishing and swimming and the girls washing the mats and the pots and pans while you walk along Effendi Alley going home. You've fished along the whole riverbank, but whenever you've gone to the river, you've done the same thing, softening up the bait in your hands, rolling up your pant legs and sitting on one of the familiar stones. Do you remember?

Twenty years had passed.

You're drunk. No, you're just angry.

When he said "Goddamn your father too!" Yusif al-Naggar was roused by the sound of a distant explosion.

Emerging from the bar onto Alfi Street, Yusif couldn't see a thing, because the lights of the cabaret marquees had been extinguished. On the way to Orabi Square, he didn't notice anyone save for the old parking attendant on the other side of the square. He headed along the sidewalk until the corner with the government bookstore and saw the storefront smashed in and the books scattered everywhere. From the tall steel birdcage, he could see the street littered with broken glass and fragments of rock. There wasn't a single storefront, window, door, or billboard that hadn't been demolished. Twenty-sixth of July Street seemed completely deserted. He could hear nothing but the occasional sound of cars speeding by, fleeing. He crossed the street and found himself in front of the public bathrooms near the Supreme Court. He hurried down the stairs and urinated. Then he headed to Ramsis Street and turned left between the Music Institute and the Telephone Building. At al-Galaa Street, he ran into a mass of people. The faççade of the al-Ahram newspaper building had been destroyed, and he heard people saying that the paper storehouses of *al-Akhbar* had been torched as well. Yusif walked along the darkened street behind al-Galaa Maternity Hospital and returned to 26th of July from the direction of Bulaq. In front of the Ali Baba Cinema, he saw the soaked, burnt shell of a bus that had been pulled into a small side street. Small children were climbing on top of it, crawling through its windows and pounding on it with rocks and iron bars. They were ripping out bolts and pieces of metal and throwing them into the road. They were ripping out the seats and throwing them through the doors. Yusif al-Naggar shuddered. From where he was standing, he could see white and brown clouds of smoke swirling around red columns of fire in front of Abu'l-Ela Bridge. He followed the long alley behind al-Sultan Mosque and came out at the Television Building along Maspero Street. The wooden billboards had been burnt, some were still hanging by their metal clamps, and some had been thrown down into the street. The flames had jumped onto the scrap wood barriers next to the new Sixth of October Bridge. Piles of tar and gravel were also on fire, sending scraps popping, exploding against fences, the edge of the sidewalk, into speeding cars. Groups of people were hurrying around warning others about the danger. He returned to the foot of the bridge and saw that the flames were leaping into the thick, green clumps of weeds growing next to the water. Heading toward Omar al-Khayyam, he glanced at the furious whirlpools of the river through the openings between the bridge's sections. Continuing on his way toward Imbaba, he realized that he hadn't seen a single soldier or bus since he'd left the Regal Bar. The glass storefronts and neon signs in Zamalek were smashed as well. The signs dangled one after another in front of the doorways, between the tree trunks and streetlight poles, and on the stones of the wide sidewalk. He passed the Officers' Club, came to the Zamalek Bridge, crossed it, and turned right along the river's edge on his way back to Kit Kat.

When he got there, he found everything just as he'd left it: the doorways lit, the fruit carts, the liver and parts carts, the coffee mill, Sadiq and his brood of children gathered around the television, the ful restaurant, Usta Badawi the barber, the department store, Khawaga's kiosk, the bookstore, Sgt. Abd al-Hamid, and the crowded doorway at the café. He walked to Hommous's to refill his butane lighter, then went to the grocery and bought another bottle of rum, putting it, wrapped in paper, in the outer pocket of his jacket. His buzz had worn off and he wanted to get drunk again. He knew he wouldn't run into anybody if he took a circuitous enough route. He crossed the street while looking at the vegetable and fruit sellers, who, sitting cross-legged with their heads wrapped in scarves, were burning a pile of shredded palm-leaf baskets. They were making tea and trying to warm themselves. And there were some people at the bus stop. Yusif al-Naggar stood directly in front of the house facing Hawa Alley, then took two steps down the stone stairs. Stepping to the right, he sat down under the squat stone wall.

He hid himself under the moist, drooping castor trees with their heavy, dark leaves and started to drink the deep red rum.

A stench was rising in the air. The breeze carried it from beyond the river, through the tall trees and over the distant houses still wet with rain.

Night of the Memorial

When the Great Haram sat next to him, Sulayman Jr. began to feel embarrassed. He got up from his seat and went to stand in the café doorway. He didn't know how much longer he should wait before going home to see if Ruwayih had returned yet. He was afraid to find that she would still be gone because that would mean he would have to go ask her mother, and in the process, admit that his wife had not come back. Qasim Effendi got up to leave because he wanted to escape having to attend the memorial service. Stopping next to Sulayman Jr., he folded the newspaper, returned it to his jacket pocket, and suggested to Sulayman that they go over to Khawaga's to sit a while. Qasim stepped off the curb and found that Sulayman was indeed coming along. Just then, he was buying a pack of cigarettes from Sgt. Abd al-Hamid and walking with him toward the other side of the street where they sat down on the chairs between Khawaga's kiosk and Usta Badawi's barber shop. Qasim Effendi said, "Give us the two best and coldest bottles of beer you can find in your iceless cooler."

Khawaga looked at them out of the corner of his eye while standing beside the kiosk and leaning with his hand on its square opening. He stretched out his hand and pressed the buttons of the cassette deck without moving from his place. Qasim Effendi took out a pack of cigarettes and gave one to Sulayman. Putting the pack into his pocket, Qasim opened the cooler himself. With a bottle in each hand he asked Khawaga, "I was wondering if you'd open these. Or should we drink them unopened? Exactly what do you expect us to do with them?"

Khawaga turned slightly, all the while looking out toward the street. He grabbed the bottle opener hanging on a string and opened the bottles while saying, as if he was addressing nobody in particular, "That comes to four bottles."

Qasim Effendi returned to his seat, and they each put their bottles under their chairs. Sulayman hadn't finished smoking his cigarette when Qasim Effendi lit another and said, "My God. You know,

Sulayman, your father, God have mercy on his soul, was a very dear friend of mine."

Sulayman Jr., however, said nothing. He'd been distracted ever since he closed up the shop and went home to watch the football game on television. Ruwayih still wasn't there. Sulayman Jr. was in his thirties but didn't have any close friends because he spent all his free time wasting his earnings at the movies. He would hardly have emerged from one cinema before he'd go into another. It was either the Cosmos, the Odeon, the Lux, or the Cairo Palace downtown, or it was the Amir in Shubra, the Marmar in Doqqi, or the Suhayr in Abbasiya.

Later, Sulayman sat by himself in his apartment. Yes, Ruwayih had really disappeared. He would wait a little while longer before going to ask her mother. The prospect annoyed him because he'd never gone there or even talked with his mother-in-law before, so Sulayman kept trying to convince himself that Ruwayih would come home after all.

Sulayman Sr. had purchased a new bedroom set several years ago, put on his black jacket with fat pockets and perched a short fez on the back of his head, its tassel falling straight down his neck. He went over to Fadlallah Osman Street and knocked on the door of a ground floor room familiar to him. He sat in front of Umm Ruwayih, who was sitting cross-legged on the other couch wearing a house robe that left her white legs exposed. He wasn't there to demand the payments she owed him. Instead, he asked her to agree to marry her daughter, Ruwayih, to his son, Sulayman Jr. He told her about how he'd bought new furniture and that from now on, if she let her daughter go, Umm Ruwayih wouldn't have to worry about what she owed. The following day, the thin Ruwayih with the arching eyebrows and dark, laughing eyes did indeed leave Fadlallah Osman Street, go down to the market, and marry Sulayman Jr.

The next morning Sulayman Sr. was late in opening his shop. For a week or ten days, he continued to open his shop quite late, and after that, people would rarely ever see him. When they did see him, he would sit downcast and everyone noticed that his health was in decline. After about a month, Sulayman Sr. died. His eyes red from crying, Sulayman Jr. appeared at the entrance of the funeral tent beaming with pride, because his Holiness Sheikh al-Tabalawi was presiding over the ceremony. Sulayman Jr. was wearing a leisure shirt, bell-bottom pants and shoes with imported, fancy rubber soles. On one of the fingers of his right hand he wore a 24-carat gold ring.

And then Sulayman Jr. proceeded to squander everything his father had left him. Unlike his father, he was not in the habit of sitting inside the store. He took his chair outside to Murad Street and sat in front of the wide storefront, where the trinkets were displayed on black and red velvet trays. He smoked a water pipe while leering at women and wouldn't bother to enter his shop unless customers came.

Today he'd gone home early in order to watch the soccer match. Since Ruwayih still wasn't home, he went to Umm Sharabat's house to see Umm Ruwayih. He introduced himself as Sulayman Jr., the son of Sulayman, the jeweler, and the husband of her daughter. Umm Ruwayih laughed and said, "I know who you are." He asked her if she knew where Ruwayih was, but she told him she didn't know a thing. When he got up to go, she asked him to let her know that Ruwayih was okay as soon as he found her, and he promised to continue searching for her. He returned to Murad Street, climbed the stairs, and went into his apartment. Not finding her there, he admitted to himself that Ruwayih must have run away. His embarrassment had prevented him from asking anybody in the neighborhood if they'd seen her. He went to the café thinking that he'd end up going downtown to the movies. He was sitting there when Qasim Effendi, the Optician, dragged him to Khawaga's kiosk to drink beer. And now, half his bottle was drained. Sulayman Jr. felt a headache coming on. He was considering leaving to see if Ruwayih had come home yet. However, Qasim Effendi produced his newspaper and began to read out the story of David Moussa, the Italian khawaga, raising his voice so Khawaga, whose back was turned to them, would hear. Qasim asked Khawaga if he understood what he was talking about. He tried to read the article aloud one more time, but Khawaga stopped him with a flick of his hand, saying angrily, "Don't go thinking you're the only one around here who knows how to read."

"Sorry. I just wanted to be sure. Of course, you know that I'm interested in your problem. In reality, it concerns us all. But then, I'm probably more interested than anybody else."

"Listen here, Amm Qasim. Calm down. Just sit there beside that guy next to you."

Khawaga left his kiosk and went over to Halawa the orange seller. Qasim Effendi laughed while closing the paper and peering at its front page, "Whoa! We're in luck! Do you see what it says here about peace, Sulayman?"

Sulayman glanced at the red banner headline and nodded his head as if to agree with what he'd just heard. Qasim Effendi continued, "Look. I've been reading *al-Ahram* all my life. Actually, I've been reading it even longer than that, because my father, God have mercy on his soul, used to read it before I was even born. Daily. You know the father of Hosna the newspaper seller? His name was Millième. He was a child back then. And by God, he'd bring us a copy of *al-Ahram* every day. Ah yes. Back when I began to despise book learning and was seduced into the world of eyeglass repair. My father divorced my mother and threw us all out of the house because he had always wanted me to get an education. When he heard from Millième that I was buying *al-Ahram* every day, he dragged me over to Hasan, the owner of the bookstore that's directly behind us here. And he tested my reading. As soon as I recited the front page of that day's paper, he took me to the neighborhood marriage official and remarried my mother immediately. And that very night all of us were back sleeping in his house. You see, my father had an immense respect for *al-Ahram* and for those who read *al-Ahram*. Just like his father before him. Unfortunately, none of my kids ever reads the paper. Once in a while, my youngest daughter looks at it to find out what's on television. But she gives it back to me quickly. But anyway, it's all right. If only it didn't beat things into the ground. Look for yourself." He pointed at the words on the page. "There's the president. There's war. There's peace. War, peace, the president. Peace, the president, war. Here's peace once more. But really now. . . ." He folded up the newspaper, "Sulayman?"

Sulayman smiled happily. His bottle was empty and he wasn't in a hurry to get home anymore. Khawaga came back. Returning the paper to his pocket and crossing his legs, Qasim Effendi said in his slow, calm voice, "Actually, if you were to ask me, I'd say that *al-Ahram* is perfectly justified in its style. It should repeat itself and use a lot of words to say what it says. Why? Because most of its readers are idiots, people who never understand what's right in front of their eyes. So, you have to grab them by the ear and tell them something over and over until it gets through their thick skulls. And sometimes God even helps them but they still don't get it. For example, take someone like that Italian khawaga. You don't need a brain to understand his situation. It's as clear as day. He has deeds that are 100 percent legal. Nowadays, you know, we go by the law. Which means he'll get his land back. All this land you see here. And then what? He's ticked off about all these houses and stores and stands here." He patted the top of the newspaper in his coat pocket. "That's what it says in the paper. Which means that as soon as he wins the preliminary trial, say goodbye to all the houses and cafés and the milkmen and oranges and steel warehouses. All of it. The mosque, the barbershop, the bookstore, the river, Sgt. Abd al-Hamid's cart, the fruit juice shop, the beer kiosks, and the liver stands. All of it. Any stand that sells beer or organs will have to go. The Italian khawaga won't leave anything standing. Why? The land belongs to him. He can build on it. He can tear everything down. He can let it go to waste or he can parcel it out. It's up to him."

He looked at Khawaga and smiled. He took a cigarette from Sulayman and lit it, saying, "Do you think we'll have to get the next two bottles for ourselves or will somebody be so generous as to get them for us? Whichever. Just let us know."

Khawaga opened the cooler, got out two bottles and said, "That makes six." Qasim Effendi placed a bottle under his seat, then composed himself and said, "So what if it's six? Or eight or a thousand? You shouldn't talk that way to your customers. Furthermore, you shouldn't talk to me in that tone. You should be ashamed. Do you think you're actually a khawaga?"

"Yes. I'm a real khawaga."

"Liar."

"What's with you, Amm Qasim?"

"You're a liar, that's what. Want to know why I say you're a liar? First of all, you're wearing a skullcap. A khawaga wouldn't wear such a thing if his life depended on it. You'd need to wear a hat with a brim. Second, you speak Arabic. Not even proper Arabic! You speak Imbaban. Khawagas don't go around speaking Imbaban. A khawaga speaks English or French or Greek. He's got to speak some kind of gibberish. You know it as well as I do. Your name isn't Jacques or Georges. It's not even Hedikoti. And furthermore, you don't know how to be polite to your customers. How could you be a khawaga? Just tell me how."

"Shut up, Amm Qasim."

"You know, you really are beautiful when you get angry. Couldn't you just marry him, Sulayman? No. You're already married. Anyway, don't get so mad. I'll help you out here. I'll explain to you how you got to be a khawaga."

"Amm Qasim . . . enough."

"You're a khawaga only because we all call you 'Khawaga.'"

"Are you through yet?"

"Of course not. We could call you 'Abduh' instead. 'Come here, Abduh. Go there, Abduh.'"

"Okay, okay. Do you have to ruin our whole evening?"

"We could do all this and more. We could call you 'Mustafa' or 'Minnie Mouse' or anything we like. We could give you one name today and change it every day or every week. It's up to us. Furthermore, this is all legal, I'll have you know. The law lets anyone call anybody whatever he likes. You couldn't make me call you 'Khawaga.' Not even the government could force me to do anything like that."

Qasim Effendi laughed and wiped some traces of beer off his mouth with the back of his hand. "But, I don't think I can call you 'Zaynab' because she is not mentioned in the law. But I promise to check this story out for you. We'll ask the government legal counsel. You know what? The law is nothing but bullshit, and God save you from getting mixed up in it!" Khawaga stared at him, fuming. Qasim Effendi went on, "I agree with you completely, it's a problem. But I'll help you solve the problem. Look, when anybody calls you something you don't like, don't respond. That's the only solution." He thought a moment and continued, "But it's a solution that'll turn out to be a little difficult. If you don't answer people, you won't sell anything, and they won't buy anything. In short, you'll be screwed. Yes, it's a real problem. That'll be a real sticking point."

Khawaga leaned into the front opening of the kiosk, took out the bills and, foaming at the mouth with rage, put the money in his vest pocket. He walked his tall frame over to the café. He sat at the doorway, crossed his legs, and took out a pack of cigarettes. He leaned his head in the door to look for Abdullah the waiter but saw the Great Haram instead. He congratulated Haram, since he thought the man would still be in jail. The police had arrested him at the café only yesterday. He said, "Nice to see you're out safely. Thank God."

"May you live long, Khawaga," said Haram.

He ordered a cup of coffee. The Great Haram was extremely pleased with himself because when they came to get him yesterday, he wasn't carrying anything incriminating on his person, unlike all the other times they'd arrested him. They'd been watching him and they stormed his house, searching it from top to bottom. But they didn't find a thing because Haram had made other arrangements.

For some time he had been going over to the house of a friend from the café, Usta Abduh, the embassy driver. They'd sit with Abduh's brazen wife Fathiya. Usta Abduh was a good enough man. While his words were scarce and infrequent, his hash smoking and smiles were constant. Only after he married Fathiya did he realize how truly outrageous she was, how she caused trouble wherever she went and trafficked in anything she could get her hands on. Late at night, Usta Abduh would take Haram home, and while they sat on the kilim in front of the bed, Fathiya put coals on the fire and made tea on a little stove perched over a stool. All the while Usta Abduh would prepare the waterpipe, and the Great Haram crumbled the hashish between his teeth and rolled the stuff into balls that he lined up along the edge of his white gallabiya. And from behind the smoke, Haram flashed Fathiya looks of repressed affection while she let him know that she understood. At first, she was content with smoking cigarettes and drinking a little beer. But after a while, she began to smoke hashish with them. But not very much.

One night, Usta Abduh, Fathiya, and Haram had smoked too much, Usta Abduh fell over and couldn't get up. With some difficulty, Haram rose and announced that he was going. Fathiya remained right where she was, sitting on the kilim. Usta Abduh finally got up and went to throw up in the toilet, thinking that perhaps vomiting would sober him up. But when he got there, he surprised the Great Haram who'd hidden himself in the toilet. He reached out and grabbed him by the neck. Abduh demanded to know whether Haram was a real man and told Haram that he knew everything and to stop making moves on his wife. Haram grabbed Usta Abduh by the throat as well. As they leaned against each other in the bathroom Haram cried out, "But we sincerely love each other and have nothing to be ashamed of, by God!" The two flew down the staircase, each still clutching the other's throat. They came out onto the alley and fell on each other, each trying to poke out the other's eyes.

The next day, when Fathiya awoke, she immediately started making a scene. She began hitting Usta Abduh with a broomstick until he ran into the alley. Then she threw his clothes out the window after him screaming, "Go to hell!" and announcing publicly how he brought people over to the house to smoke hashish. Usta Abduh gathered up his clothes. He looked up at Fathiya, who was hanging out of the window, swearing that she was divorced from him.

The Great Haram began negotiations with Fathiya from afar, and then started to visit her secretly at night, long after the alley had gone to sleep. He'd leave his baggies and scale with her, paying her three pounds each day for her services.

Whenever the police detective yanked him from the café and dragged him to search his house, he could never find anything incriminating. Still when the detective took him to the station and warned him to stop dealing dope, the Great Haram swore that, for the past three or four months, he'd given up his old ways. However, when the police informants assured the detective that Haram had not stopped selling hashish, the detective felt his only remaining option was to try to make him cooperate in the investigation of a couple of other suspected dealers. Haram swore he'd do his best but never actually did anything to help, because he wasn't about to help the authorities catch his associates.Anything but that! The last time they saw each other, the detective asked Haram about how the case was going. Haram replied that since he'd stopped dealing drugs, he'd lost touch with those elements and now didn't know who was buying and who wasn't, "Our Lord is great. I'm a believer in that. God willing, I'll keep looking into it for you." The detective told him that if he didn't stop selling drugs and help out with the investigation like they'd agreed upon, he'd trump up charges against Haram, charges that would put him behind bars for at least two years.

So they had arrested him yesterday, and the officer stood him in front of the informants and took out a napkin with a small bundle of hashish from his desk drawer. From a different drawer, he took out a pocketknife with a gazelle-horn handle. While he filled out the report, he said that at 9 p.m., they had apprehended Haram who was sitting outside Awadullah's café, selling narcotic substances. In the right pocket of his vest, they found a large white napkin with ten pieces of hashish inside, wrapped in blue cellophane, ready for sale. A pocketknife was found in the left side pocket of his gallabiya. The Great Haram thought he was royally screwed. That night in the holding cell, however, he came to an agreement with one of the prisoners who was due to be released the next morning. They exchanged clothing. When he was taken before the magistrate, Haram stood there wearing a T-shirt and blue jeans that were much too short for him. And, due to the long underwear he was wearing underneath, they were much too tight as well. When the prosecutor finished looking over the evidence register and the police report, he looked at Haram in disbelief and asked, "So where're the clothes?"

"What clothes, sir?"

"The clothes mentioned in the report. The gallabiya and vest?"

"How would I know, sir? This is what I was wearing when they arrested me." They searched the cell and looked at the outfits of the other prisoners. They interrogated the guards who worked the night shift. They beat him and turned the place inside out. But they didn't find the gallabiya and vest. And so the prosecutor had to release him. The Great Haram slept all day at his first wife's house, then woke up and went to the café. This made Abdullah uneasy, and he would not let Haram out of his sight. Abdullah watched Haram approach Maallim Atiya. They exchanged some words which Abdullah wasn't able to hear. Abdullah followed Haram when he went outside to sit with Khawaga. Again, he tried to catch what they said, but they didn't talk at all. He rushed over to the alley between the café and the basement apartment when he saw Haram walking toward Maallim Sobhi's shop. He sat on the ground next to the sheep and turkeys, so he could peer into the open window of the office, where he saw the Great Haram walking between the cages. Haram stopped in front of Maallim Sobhi, who was thinking about something, his head resting on his chest. Abdullah heard the voice of the Great Haram say, "Good evening."

Maallim Sobhi was startled to see Haram. He figured that the man was still in jail. "Oh! Thank God, you were released!" he said.

"Thanks. God bless you."

"Coffee or tea?"

"No. Money."

"What money?"

"Two hundred pounds. The rest of the price of the building."

"What are you talking about, Haram? Oh all right, but you're going to need to be patient. By the next time you see me, I'll have it."

"You already have it now."

"What about Atiya and the café?"

"That's between you and Atiya. I had an agreement. Sheikh Hosni sold and I bought. Then I sold and you bought, and that settles that. It's over."

"What do you mean bought and sold? Did you pay any money, Haram?"

"Yeah. I paid what I had to. What's more, I just got out of jail, and I've got expenses, court costs, and work to worry about. Or should I just act crazy and make a scene? And why don't we take it to court while we're at it?"

"What do you mean, Haram?"

"Just what I said."

"Be reasonable."

"What do you expect me to do? You're trying to piss me off."

"Sit down, then." He leaned over and opened the iron safe, "See, I'm no deadbeat. Here you go."

"There you go. You're finally getting smart. Now you handle Atiya. Goodbye."

Abdullah remained sitting with the sheep and the turkeys, unable to get up. At times he thought he was imagining all this. Only now did he realize that it was for real and that the deal had already been closed. He was completely overcome with grief.

The Great Haram walked out, crossed the street, and bought a couple of packs of cigarettes from Sgt. Abd al-Hamid. Abdullah couldn't move from where he was. Haram hurried out to Murad Street and from there toward Fadlallah Osman. Looking up and down the street, he passed through Qatr al-Nada until he came to the short, dark Tawakkul Alley. He went inside the building at the end. Haram slipped past the ground floor room.

Abdullah still couldn't move.

Haram went up the steps, his feet making no sound, he walked past the toilet on the uncovered portion of the roof. He tapped on the locked door three times and then once more. The sound of the bolt opening was heard, and he turned the handle and entered the apartment.

Abdullah, still sitting next to the open window, began to feel a pain in his legs. He was afraid that people would think he was squatting, shitting among the sheep and turkeys. So he stood up and walked from the alley to the middle of the street. He stood there for a moment, then hurried off to Amir. He leaned over and told Amir what he'd just seen, then went to Sgt. Abd al-Hamid to inform him too. He found the sergeant staring silently at Khawaga. Seeing an empty chair next to him, Abdullah sat on it and said to himself, "What's the use? He already knows everything." With the sergeant, he stared at Khawaga who'd left his kiosk and was still sitting by himself in the café's doorway even though he'd finished his coffee.

Sulayman Jr. approached Khawaga and paid his beer tab. Then, tipsy, he staggered down Murad Street. Qasim Effendi had already escaped: when Khawaga went to the café, he stood up with his short, thin body, and said, raising his finger and leaning over, "Pardon me, Mr. Sulayman. Give me four minutes. I'm going to the toilet and then I'm coming right back." Eagerly, he stepped off the curb and hurried away. Sulayman Jr. looked and saw Qasim Effendi walking away and took advantage of the moment to finish his third bottle and go to the café. He paid Abdullah and Khawaga what he owed them. He wasn't conscious of what he was doing until he reached his building, walked up the stairs, and stood in front of his apartment and saw that the lights were off. He looked for a match in his pocket. Unable to find one, he pulled out his key. Suddenly, while he was trying to find the keyhole, he became afraid and hurried, almost falling, downstairs. He came out into the cold air again and felt revived. He wandered around until he got tired. He went through Qatr al-Nada to Fadlallah Osman and to the building where Umm Sharabat lived. He looked out of the corner of his eye while he walked along and saw that Umm Ruwayih's window was closed and the light was off. He said to himself that she'd gone to sleep. And that even if the window had been open, he wouldn't have been able to knock on her door and ask her about Ruwayih because she would have figured out that he was drunk, "Which in itself isn't anything. But maybe I would end up mixing up my words while talking." He realized that he was approaching Gaber's grocery shop. Gaber was leaning out, talking to Faruq and Shawqi who were there standing in front. When Sulayman Jr. realized they'd seen him, he felt that he couldn't go back in the direction he was coming from, since that might lead them to think that he was looking for Ruwayih who'd disappeared. Or something like that. The best thing for him to do would be to keep going and buy a pack of cigarettes. Then he could go back.

Gaber stopped talking and Faruq stood up, saying, "Do you know who that is who's walking toward us?"

Shawqi was quick to say, "Would you believe it? That's Sulayman, the jeweler."

"And he's really drunk."

"Really?"

"I swear. I saw him drinking beer at Khawaga's."

"Look at that jerk. He didn't even contribute money for the funeral."

Sulayman Jr. was on the short side. He wore a wide belt with a round metal buckle around his ample girth. Raising a finger to his chin, he said, "Good evening, gentlemen." When they returned his greetings, he rested his elbow on the marble countertop and began to look at the shelves of goods. He asked if there were any Cleopatra cigarettes and Gaber said, "We've got some."

Shawqi said, "We've got beer too."

Faruq added, "Sit down and rest."

He took him by the hand to the darkened storehouse across from the shop and sat him down on one of the empty soda cartons. Patting him gently he said, "You sit down. I'll bring you the cigarettes."

Sulayman, trying to put his hand in his pocket, said, "Here. Take some money too."

Shawqi said, "No sir! Don't insult us like that. You want a couple bottles of beer? Gaber, get us two bottles. No, make it three." Gaber opened the bottles of beer. Faruq carried them over and sat in front of Sulayman and put the bottles on the ground. Shawqi brought over some black olives, Romano cheese, and pieces of bread and joined them, saying, "I hope you don't mind but we don't have any beer glasses."

Sulayman raised his hand a little, then let it fall. Then he said, "We're neighborhood boys. Always have been. I just drank six beers with Qasim Effendi. Without any glasses. It's perfectly normal to drink this beer. Even without this finger food you see here."

Faruq agreed and told Shawqi that Sulayman was one of "those really good guys, you know." And they began to drink their beer.

After ditching Sulayman, Qasim Effendi had taken a long detour, hoping that his companion would take the opportunity to pay his tab. He came to Fadlallah Osman Street, stopped in front of Gaber's shop, and whispered, "Good evening there."

"Nice evening to you, Amm Qasim," said Gaber.

"What do you think, Gaber? I'm feeling pretty good right now. Really good, actually."

"You've been feeling good your entire life, Amm Qasim."

"Okay. As long as I'm feeling good, whaddaya say we have another bottle? One nice bottle. We drink it. We share some nice conversation. Or, should I just go on feeling good like I am? Any reason to drink more? Whaddaya think?"

"The truth is, it's all kind of confusing."

"So then you probably want me to go over to the café. One last cup of coffee. One sugar. One of those choice Florida cigarettes. Then to the memorial service. And then to sleep. Whaddaya say, Gaber?" When he became aware of movement behind him in the storehouse doorway, he turned toward Shawqi and Faruq and Sulayman and, seeing only the first two, he turned back to Gaber and said, "Hi." He headed to the café and saw Abdullah sitting on a chair next to Sgt. Abd al-Hamid, and asked, "What's this, Abdullah? You patronize this place too?" He turned and saw Khawaga and sat next to him without greeting him or saying anything. He clapped his hands and said, "Make it one without sugar, Abdullah."

Abdullah got up and left Sgt. Abd al-Hamid staring at Khawaga. The sergeant was thinking that if anything were to happen to the café, it would be a catastrophe for him too. He sat at the café on account of his friends who were regulars there. Most people bought their smokes from Khawaga. But the sergeant's sales had risen lately since Khawaga had been caught selling a pack of cigarettes for more than its stipulated price, and the government cut off his supply of tobacco for six months. The sergeant never considered himself a cigarette vendor. He sat there next to the café drinking tea like any customer enjoying the company of his old friends, who frequented the place and took their chairs over by him, even if they didn't always talk with him. He'd go crazy if the café were to close and he had to sit alone on the sidewalk selling cigarettes. He wished that either he didn't have these friends or that they sat together in a different place, one that wasn't in danger of closing. Then he wished that he'd never come to Imbaba or ever met these people at all.

Many years had passed since he took a leave of absence to get married and then returned to the police station. He began to notice that his bride would go into the bathroom for an hour or more at a time. As he always did before he got married, he woke up in the morning and went to the bathroom. But he would find that she'd have gotten there before him. He paced back and forth between the bedroom and the living room, feeling a sharp pain gathering under his belly. He'd busy himself putting on his socks and regulation shoes. He'd shave, trying but unable to keep still in front of the mirror. Finally, when he thought that he'd be late for work, he would take off his gallabiya, and throw it on the mat spread in front of the bed with the long black posts and print bedspread. Putting on his regulation winter uniform, he hurried out the door, trying to reach the regulation toilets at the station before he exploded. What depressed him was something he noticed later. He'd wake up in the morning, put on his clogs and go into the living room where he'd see her. And before he could say, "Good morning", she'd have finished whatever she was doing and beaten him to the toilet. Abd al-Hamid thought hard and decided it was unthinkable that his beautiful wife did all that intentionally. However, not finding an explanation for the coincidence, which happened routinely, he thought that anybody who'd do that on purpose was inhuman and insensitive. But what about his wife? He was amazed to see her coming out of the bathroom with her soft, beautiful face and eyes, and her tired, sweet smile. The few times that she came out before he left for work, he was so embarrassed to be seen hurrying toward the toilet in front of her that he'd feign, walking slowly even while he was about to lose it. He never found the courage to discuss the problem with her, nor with anybody else for that matter. When he resigned himself to the fact that he'd never be able to draw her attention to his problem, he buried the secret in his bosom and began to cultivate a profound hatred toward her in his heart.

And he changed his hours to the night shift. He started sleeping during the day and retrieving his rifle from the station before he went on his nightly rounds. The sergeant said that those days were the best and that if only he were able to predict what might happen, he would never be surprised by anything.

He was the only one to see the knife attack on Maallim Atiya because from where he was sitting he had a clear view of the café, the alley, and the shop. He saw the Maallim fall to his knees, holding onto the wall for support and clutching his side. The sergeant was about to get up, but he noticed Maallim Atiya jump to his feet and adjust his clothes. The Maallim then ran over to the doorway of the café, talked with Abdullah in a calm voice, and left. He knew that the Maallim was hiding whatever it was that had happened. After the Maallim walked away, he called Abdullah over and told him what he had just seen. But Abdullah said that the Maallim had just been there and that there was nothing noticeably wrong with him. It just wasn't possible.

The sergeant smiled later when poor Abdullah confirmed the incident upon seeing the Great Haram going to Maallim Sobhi's to collect the rest of his bill. He turned to look at Abdullah sitting next to him. When Abdullah noticed and his eyes met Abd al-Hamid's now bulging eyes, he shuddered suddenly, thinking that this wasn't the Abd al-Hamid he knew. Abdullah stood up and hurried over to the café which was now crowded. He saw Qasim Effendi sitting among them, holding open a newspaper and reading a story out loud about the knife attack on Maallim Atiya as if it were written about a stranger like the Italian khawaga. Abdullah was surprised to see that the whole café already knew about the incident. He looked at Maallim Atiya and found him laughing, playing with the copper tokens on the plate. Noticing that the maallim was in a pretty good mood, Abdullah decided to talk with him. He stood in front of the counter, waiting for the coffee without sugar that Qasim Effendi had ordered. "Hey, Maallim, did you hear about that thing with the Italian khawaga in the paper?"

The maallim remained silent for a moment then muttered, "You're very interested in khawaga news these days, aren't you?"

"Well, it's just that the Italian khawaga thing seems important, Maallim. He's trying to get his hands on the whole neighborhood. Maybe you should have waited a little while longer before thinking about leaving the café."

"You're a real jackass. First, you tell me a khawaga is going to get the whole neighborhood, then you want me to wait?"

Abdullah was shocked. What the maallim had said was and was not correct. He felt like he'd just lost everything. The maallim smiled and said, "And why are you getting so involved? You're the one who started it all, you idiot!"

The maallim turned to a customer, and said, "Really, it's the truth. That Sobhi started his fortune with a lottery ticket that cost two piasters. Our friend Abdullah here would earn twenty-five piasters every day from me. And then he'd go spend fifteen piasters of it on lottery tickets. He did that habitually because the first time he ever bought a ticket, he won a pound and took home eighty-five piasters profit! After that he was hooked. I swear. He wasted his money and all his hard work on those lottery tickets until he'd spent everything. It was useless! Anyway, one day, I was sitting and he was standing in front of me just like he is now. And in comes Mounir, the lottery ticket kid, with one ticket left to sell. He gives it to Abdullah. But that idiot got it into his head that he couldn't buy it. The boy tries to give the ticket to someone else, but that one wouldn't take it either. Just then, Sobhi, the chicken man, walks in the door. In those days he had no shop. He had been squatting for a month or two peddling his chickens in front of the café. So guess what happens? He comes in to have some tea. He wasn't thinking of anything in particular. He sees Mr. Shit here saying that he can't take the ticket, and Sobhi grabs it, puts it in his pocket, takes out two piasters from his turban, gives it to the boy, and leaves. And our all-hearing and all-knowing God decides that that's the ticket that will win the grand prize. Two hundred pounds. With the winnings from that very same ticket, Sobhi went and paid for that basement shop that he's in now. Then he bought this building, and the one behind it, and the one behind that too, I'll have you know. I'm not objecting, of course, everyone is entitled to their share. But more importantly, what's happened since then? Note the difference between God's creations. Let's see. Who's smarter here? One guy plays the lottery once and wins a pound and takes home eighty-five piasters, then wastes his life going after the grand prize. Why? Because he's an idiot, that's why. Another guy plays the lottery once, wins the grand prize and then stops playing immediately. Why? Because he's smart." He turned to Abdullah and nodded smiling, "Watch out. God did that to teach you a special lesson. But do you ever learn? Go back to work. Get out of here."

The man who had been listening flashed a smile and said, "Anyway, it's all for the best, Maallim. Even if Abdullah had bought that ticket, it would have turned out a loser."

Abdullah always put the lottery ticket story out of his mind, never remembering it unless someone else brought it up. But the thing he could never forget and always talked about was how he was standing in front of the café one Thursday when Sobhi first appeared at the café carrying a cage with three chickens inside. Sobhi asked him for permission to sit in front of the café and sell his birds, and Abdullah obliged him. Abdullah would always say that he welcomed Sobhi because it was a question of letting a man earn his living. Before that, Sobhi had been sitting in a patch of dirt in Kit Kat Square. Sobhi hadn't finished his first cup of tea when his business took off, and he wanted to sit on one of the café's chairs. And now he had an office and a steel safe. Abdullah would say that he didn't hate him. They even might have remained friends if Sobhi hadn't started all the trouble. Sobhi stopped ordering his own tea. Instead, he started sending a young boy to get it for him and to tell Abdullah to come by and fetch the tray and the tab. Abdullah braced himself and began to counter-attack. He refused to retrieve the tray and would tell the messenger, "I said, be patient, boy. Maybe he's not ready to close his tab. Anyway, the tray's not going anywhere." That was in the hopes that Sobhi would act like a decent human being and send over the tray and what he owed. But Sobhi didn't do that. At the end of the night, Maallim Atiya took inventory of everything: the chairs, the cups, the waterpipes, the plates and spoons, everything. And the money, of course, down to the last millième. Abdullah left the café angrily, headed to the alley and stood in front of the window and began to call for Sobhi. The new boy came out and asked Abdullah to come downstairs because the Maallim wanted him. Abdullah went inside and down stairs he'd never gone down before. Walking between crates of live chickens, he entered and found Maallim Sobhi sitting behind a wooden desk. He was busy counting a pile of money that sat behind the tray and tea cups. As soon as he stopped counting, Sobhi asked him about the bill and then handed the money to him, saying, "Here you are."

Abdullah, sitting like the other customers, one leg resting on the other, repeated, "'Here you are.' I accepted his tip. If I'd only refused it from the beginning, I could have stopped him in his tracks. He wouldn't have bought the building and taken over the café. He wouldn't have become a Maallim or anything. That's what started it! 'Here you are.'" Abdullah looked over and saw Maallim Sobhi standing outside his shop in front of a truck loaded with chicken crates. He thought about going over to talk to him, and he imagined for a second that the Maallim might even be nice to him, "Maybe I haven't been fair to him." They didn't have any misunderstandings between them about buying and selling. The real conflict was between him and Maallim Atiya. Then he realized that what had transpired had benefited both maallims. Why? Maallim Sobhi's dealings were perfectly above board. He'd bought a dirt cheap café in a great location. Maallim Atiya had sold a café that didn't really belong to him. The Great Haram had profited on the deal most of all. All of them gained something. As for himself, what could he say? Abdullah couldn't work or be a waiter except in Awadullah's café.

"You see, this café you're in became a café at the same time I became a waiter," he told a customer, "Together. I still remember back when Amir was born, when Ahmad was born, when Ibrahim Sr. was born. Think about when Hagg Awadullah was Ibrahim's age, imagine him at Ahmad's age, or Amir's age. Damn! I've been here longer than even I can remember. In sum, without Awadullah's café, there's no Abdullah." What would he do then? When he got up in the morning and couldn't come here, where would he go? How would he survive? If Maallim Atiya had acted virtuously, he would have to talk with him, since the maallim could hold onto the café. But Maallim Atiya sold the café and it wasn't even his to sell. "He sold me out and sold everybody out. God damn you too, Sheikh Hosni!" Abdullah rose and walked over to Maallim Sobhi who was supervising the unloading of the truck. Abdullah wanted to do something for the sake of the café, for the sake of everyone. If only the Italian khawaga had appeared before he bought the building, he could have scared the maallim, "I wouldn't buy if I were you! That khawaga is going to snatch up everything." However, now Abdullah was in no position to dissuade the maallim from buying because the purchase had already been made. For that reason, Abdullah was going to ask him not to hurry, to leave things as they were, to leave the building and the café as they were until the government finished looking into the matter. "I'm saying this for the general good. You know I don't stand to profit one way or another. I'm just scared that you're going to tear things down and spend your money on building and then the khawaga will win his court case, and it'd be a real tragedy," he told Sobhi.

The maallim didn't respond. Instead, he stood in front of the scales and recorded the weight of each crate in his notebook. One of the tall boys working for the maallim approached Abdullah and rudely pushed him on the shoulders, saying, "Aren't you scared that the truck will go into reverse and crush you under the wheels?"

Abdullah looked toward Maallim Sobhi as he said to the boy, "Get your hands off me!"

But the maallim's boy pushed him again and said that if he wanted to die, he should go somewhere else to do it. Maallim Atiya limped up, stood in the doorway of the café, and asked Abdullah if he had become a thug, "Or what's the deal here?" During all this, Maallim Sobhi never raised his head. "It's true," thought Abdullah to himself, "When treachery rules, safety is cheap. When dishonesty has its way, it rules without mercy. It's true, you've been pitiful all your life." He turned to enter the café. Just then, he ran into Sheikh Hosni standing there, soaking wet and covered with mud. Maallim Ramadan rushed out from inside screaming, "What a hellish day, what happened to you?" Qasim Effendi stood up as did Usta Sayyid Tilib, so did Abd al-Khaliq, the undertaker, and Usta Qadri English and everyone else who was there. Even Amm Omran raised his head and tried to figure out the scene. Sheikh Hosni was standing in the doorway of the café, his legs shivering, a pool of water forming under his feet. "What are you all looking at?" he asked.

Qasim Effendi fired back, "Don't worry about it, maestro. They've just never seen someone sweating before. You must've been jogging or something."

After deliberately knocking into Maallim Ramadan and smudging his gallabiya, the sheikh headed immediately for the inside corner of the café. When everyone rose with Usta Qadri English to begin the night of mourning, he remained there, still sitting. Amm Omran also ignored them. Before Sheikh Hamada al-Abiad was to begin reciting a few suras from the Qur'an, they sent for Faruq to switch on the sound system. And they went on talking about the Italian khawaga and Mrs. Ouda Pasha and Kit Kat and Maallim Sobhi. Qasim Effendi held up the folded newspaper and said that if the khawaga won the case, the maallim would be done for.

Chapter
Eleven

EARLIER, USTA QADRI English had been standing in the entrance of his apartment, welcoming everyone as they arrived for the memorial service for Amm Migahid. The Usta had raced ahead in order to stand here, greeting them and looking intently into their eyes. He searched for signs of whether they knew about the stolen calf's head, but he was unable to grasp their thoughts. He treated them with due solemnity and didn't respond to a single smile or word with more than what was necessary. With time, he relaxed, comforted by the thought that none of them had ever known a thing. He shrugged off those lethal fears, cursing the devil, his insanity, and the whole world. He began to feel an outpouring of love for all those present. And he realized that Umm Abduh, who had raged and cursed him when he told her about their hosting the service, was only motivated by her excessive concern about the cleanliness of the house that would be thrown into disarray by all those mourners. Like him, most likely she also felt that it would be inviting bad luck to have the service at their house. He started to look at everybody in a new way, supposing that what had happened was just a coincidence. He remembered that Desdemona had also been innocent. He had known that all along. The handkerchief had been misplaced. It was Emilia who stole it and gave it to Iago who then stuck it in Cassio's room. He scoffed at the English prudishness he was so affected by, then considered it a dead-end path. The Usta turned and smiled at the father of Sheikh Hamada al-Abiad, who was sitting cross-legged on the sofa in front of the tilting microphone stand whose base was being held in place by his single black shoe. The sheikh was in his early twenties. He was rocking back and forth to the movement of the prayer beads running through the fingers of his hand. His hand rested on his knee folded under a jubba that opened to reveal a shiny caftan. His face was the color of salt, imbued with a redness at the tips of the ears and cheeks. Under the edge of his fez, his sideburns, his thin eyebrows and his long eyelashes, appeared as fine, silver lines. Sheikh Hamada al-Abiad was the son of Sudanese parents. His father worked at the Semiramis Hotel and liked to have a good time. One night, he came home drunk, climbed upstairs and found Nafisa, his wife, in the process of giving birth to his first son. So he went downstairs, sat with Amm Muhammad Hasan, Gaber's father, and drank three bottles of cold beer before they finally told him that she'd finished giving birth. When he went upstairs for the second time, he saw a baby so white it looked like a little sun had popped out of the body of Nafisa, who was the very daughter of blackness itself. He sobered up immediately, swearing to divorce her. Then the next day when people told him he'd been ungrateful to God, he let her come back. But the next year, when she gave birth to a black girl he announced again he would divorce her, only to take her back once more.

He began to think of Hamada as a white miracle walking around on two small legs, grabbing onto the legs of chairs, the edge of the sofa, crawling on the mat, crying, laughing, nursing, getting sick, growing teeth, producing excrement, looking at his father, recognizing him, saying, "Daddy's home," and smiling. He saw the miracle walk by itself along the wall, bending its skinny neck, lifting its short gallabiya to expose skinny, ivory-white legs, and raising its hand to shield its eyes from the light of the sun. The father was pleased with himself and with the world and with Nafisa, but then he'd get drunk and forget everything about it.

Usta Qadri began to mingle with the mourners, looking natural and saying to himself that he was like a sick person on the road to health. He saw Faruq walk in and start up the loudspeaker system. He was startled to see that Zaghlul the parts seller had come to the service. The Usta shook his slimy hand while Zaghlul wiggled his eyebrows that had been trimmed by Usta Sayyid Tilib the Barber. Usta Qadri saw his laughing, depraved eyes and almost threw a violent fit. Instead, he left his house and the service, intending not to return until after Sheikh Hamada finished reciting the Qur'an, until all those in the group, and especially that disgusting Zaghlul, had left his house. The sheikh began to clear his throat and tap his finger on the microphone until everyone became completely silent.

When he began to recite the Sura of the Merciful, Faruq got up to leave. He went out to the street and looked to make sure that Sulayman and Shawqi were still at the storehouse. He headed toward Amir al-Giyush Alley and went inside his building where he told his mother that he was still busy with the work of supervising the big memorial service for Amm Migahid that they'd put together in Kit Kat Square. He went to the bathroom, pushed through the tight wooden door and pissed on the wall so as not to splatter the hem of his pants. Then he turned and said to his mother that he was going out again because that loudspeaker she could hear reciting the Qur'an right now had been entrusted to him. He had borrowed it with a receipt, and he was responsible for returning it. He went out into the alley buttoning his pants when he bumped into Fatma who was just returning. She asked him, "What's with you? You drunk or something?"

Faruq smiled, approached, and told her that she was coming home awfully early. He put his hand on her arm and asked her if that was a new shirt she was wearing.

Fatma smiled and walked away, then turned and went into her building. She was still smiling, happy about the circumstances which had worked in her favor: she was glad she hadn't seen Yusif after she'd had time to think about things and came to realize that if she'd gone with him to his friend's apartment, he would have slept with her only to prove his manhood. Then he would have ditched her. She thought about it on the bus. When she imagined herself taking off her clothes in a strange place, she shuddered because she'd never been naked outside of Imbaba. She thought to herself that the best way would be to meet him and tell him that she was busy and couldn't go with him to his friend's apartment. Then they could return to Imbaba together. And if, after that, he still wanted to sleep with her, she would take him to the ground floor apartment. He might fail again and keep after her just to prove that he could indeed have sex with her. When she got off the bus, she'd already made up her mind. Downtown, she stood waiting for him, content with herself because she'd found this solution to her problem. Then she heard the noisy demonstration and got scared. She walked back and got on a bus without seeing Yusif. After she'd put some distance between herself and downtown and gotten closer to Imbaba, she was able to relax. And she thought that circumstances had been kind to her. If he asked her why she wasn't there, she could tell him that she came to meet him but things were so crazy that she decided to go home immediately.

Fatma waltzed through the door of her apartment and found her mother sitting with Umm Ruwayih in front of the bathroom. "Good evening," she said taking off her shoes and skirt. She went into the toilet, took off the rest of her clothes and, without closing the door, squatted to urinate in front of the two women. She burst out laughing, "And what do you think you're looking at?" The two women laughed when she came out. She opened her purse, took out some small bags of snuff and gave them to her mother. She offered her mother a cigarette and lit one for herself. She put on her sandals, walked out of the house, and paused at the door. She was wearing a wool shirt and a red silk pajama top that came down to the middle of her bronze thighs. Holding her cigarette, she leaned against the wall and looked into Yusif's window, but the light wasn't on. She realized that he wasn't home and said in a loud voice, "How're you doing, Grocer, you son of a bitch?" Gaber turned in her direction but remained silent for a moment. Then he said that, in any case, he wasn't going to respond. She snorted, spat, and said, "And tell me, why not?" She sauntered toward them in her camisole shirt with her hair undone, "Good evening, gentlemen."

Sulayman, taken aback, blurted out, "Good evening to you"

She walked over to the shop doorway and, leaning on the marble countertop to talk to Gaber, she turned her back to the others. The backs of her ample thighs were in full view. Faruq looked and winked. But Sulayman, who could open his eyes only with great difficulty, didn't see anything. Then he heard her hoarse laugh and raised his head to see her walking away, swinging her hips while she headed into Amir al-Giyush Alley and disappeared without turning around. Faruq said, "So, whaddaya think?"

Sulayman nodded his heavy head but didn't answer.

"You in the mood?"

Listlessly, Sulayman said, "You must be kidding."

Shawqi said that Faruq could help him get to her place. With the same relaxed tone, Sulayman said that he was ready to pay any amount, "Gaber, I'll give him fifty pounds."

Faruq said not now. They'd have to make arrangements first and it'd be best if they cracked open a beer for her. When Sulayman agreed, Faruq suggested that they make it two bottles of beer and one of tonic so that she'd get tipsy. He leaned over in Shawqi's ear and whispered in a loud voice. Sulayman heard him saying "Fatma" and that they'd have to help Sulayman since he was such a good guy. Faruq asked Gaber not to forget the cheese and olives and he got up and took two bottles of beer and a big one of tonic, and the package of white cheese and Romano cheese and the black olives and he turned to walk toward the alley. Sulayman, suddenly afraid, said, "God! You're not really going over there, are you?"

"Sure am."

Sulayman turned to Shawqi and said, "As you are my witness, I have nothing to do with this."

"Okay."

"It's just that I'm sitting here with you, trying to get up and go home."

When he saw Faruq return, he tried to get out of his seat, but Faruq told him, "It's done."

"You mean you told her?"

"Shame on you for even asking."

"Do you swear?"

"Come on . . . be a man."

"Did she listen to what you had to say?"

Shawqi said, "He's telling you, 'it's done.' That means it's a done deal." They continued drinking.

The second time Faruq returned from Amir al-Giyush alley, he was carrying four empty bottles of beer. He sat down and said, "Sulayman. Whaddaya say? Tonight, I want you to sleep with Fathiya. Forget about Fatma."

Sulayman lifted his head with difficulty and said, "Who?"

"Fathiya."

Shawqi said, "Fathiya? Oh my God, she's gorgeous!"

Faruq asked Shawqi to go arrange things with Fathiya. While Shawqi walked off, Sulayman said angrily, "But I wanted the other one."

Faruq told him that Fathiya was really Fatma and that he could call her whatever name he wished. Faruq said that he didn't tell him that earlier because he didn't want Shawqi to find out and go sleep with her. Gaber jumped out of the shop doorway and told them that he had to leave shortly to get the milk and yogurt from Zamalek. Faruq told him that they would be going to take care of some important business with their friend Sulayman and that they'd come back to wait for him later. Gaber looked at Sulayman and said that no offense but since he was there, he might as well collect what they owed now. While he was adding things up and taking Sulayman's money, Shawqi pissed in the alley and returned staggering, still buttoning his fly. Faruq asked, "Done?"

"Let's go."

But Sulayman couldn't stand up. Shawqi and Faruq pulled him up by the arms until he stood. They walked him away, "Look. You'll go into the first alley on the left. Then go into the first alley on the right. Tawakkul Alley. It's the building at the end. Go right inside."

"Who will?"

"You will."

"How?"

"Straight ahead."

Shawqi said, "That's right, straight on in."

Sulayman's legs turned in one direction while his torso spun in the opposite. Faruq twisted him back into place, and they walked Sulayman over to the end of Tawakkul Alley, which was completely dark. Faruq whispered that it was the building at the very end. Shawqi assured him he'd be waiting right there. When Sulayman began to shuffle his feet forward, the two others walked backwards. Sulayman was leaning unsteadily forward, his arms stretched out as far as they could reach, his mouth wide open. He stumbled forward until he reached the house at the end of the narrow pitch-black alley. The window of the ground floor was shut tight although a thin stream of light slipped out through the pieces of cardboard covering the shutter's gaps from the inside. Leaning his hands on the window frame, he put his face close and tried to look inside. The two others peddled backwards, hid themselves, and finally ran away, laughing hysterically until they reached the café. However, since they couldn't find an empty seat, they had to stand in the middle of the street. Shawqi ordered two cups of tea from Abdullah and pointed to the place they were going to sit. Next to the mosque wall, behind Sgt. Abd al-Hamid and Amir Awadullah, they sat on the base of the stone wall and took their teas from Abdullah who, carrying the tray, angrily asked them if either of them was going to want a glass of water too. Then he turned around before either could answer. When he walked off the curb, Amir noticed him and said, "Where's my coffee, Abdullah?" And then Amir went back to staring over there.

Everybody who usually came to the café was there. Maybe one or two were missing, but the basic shape of each clique was complete. Some of them had gone to the memorial service, some of them had come back. They were the offspring of Imbaba's side streets and thoroughfares. Did any of them know that this would be the last night they'd spend in their café? Amir noted that Maallim Atiya was an idiot. He could have purchased the building and everything would have continued as it was. He could have bought it before Maallim Sobhi did. Amir stopped thinking about it since thoughts like these made him sad. He wanted to find a different way of thinking about it. If he could do that, he'd feel more relaxed. But he didn't know how. Contemplating it further, he thought that, as Yusif al-Naggar would say, a person really needed to get out of his own skin in order to see things. He had tried doing that, but without success. No. How, while sitting right now in the café, could he see what the days and months and years had stolen? Just how? He arrived at the café at the beginning of the day so that nothing would escape him. And he never left it. He tried to remember what it looked like when he was young, when he used to come with his father, and he realized he was trying to do the impossible. Amir thought, you must have been a toddler like any other, sucking at your mother's breast, laughing, crying, and pronouncing your first words. And your father, Hagg Awadullah, liked to carry you in his arms sometimes, hugging you tight, rocking you in your crib while he paced back and forth, trying to stop your crying and get you to sleep, just like you do now with your son Abdullah. If Abdullah were grown, he'd bring him here to see the café that bore his grandfather's name, Awadullah. But even if his son were to see the café now, he wouldn't remember it. The tie has been cut: the café is gone, Awadullah is gone. Today is the day your father died. He began to remember more distant times. Kit Kat and its giant stone entrance, the writing on the lofty arch: "The battle of the Pyramids took place here on the 21st of July, 1798." Abdullah brought his coffee, lingered for a while, then walked off. Amir recalled the day he'd cried on account of Kit Kat. He knew that the contractor had purchased the rubble of the Kit Kat club. When he returned from work, he saw the massive, shiny stones split into pieces, strewn along the empty plot of land behind it at the entrance to the city of Imbaba. He stood in a corner of the square looking at the square tables draped with white cloth that hung down to the deep green grass. And the bushes with candles hidden inside, giving off light like so many small moons. And how so often at night he'd climb the camphor tree with his playmates. Here was the royal winter hall. On its roof, supported by marble columns topped with capitals, was another wooden roof around which hung intricately designed eaves. This was where the king would go during the summer. He looked and saw the king's private entrance with its heavy, brass knocker.

Amir remembered how during the war, they stood there watching the Allied soldiers stationed in Kit Kat, near the guava orchards, and on the houseboats. The Black soldiers gazed back at them from on top of the winter hall, from the tall stone entrance, from behind the barbed wire around the orchards. They called out, "We're Muslims too!" and threw chocolate bars and heavy pocketknives with rough, black handles which the kids would exchange for a few piasters and spend the money on soft drinks . . . . Muhammad Atiya bought a tire from them and purchased knives from the kids. Hamama would come with his brother and brother-in-law Salama and they'd stand under the winter hall yelling, "Giff me won sigaret, Mr. Khawaga!" The Great Haram hid his drugs under a tree in the guava orchard. And they walked past the seller of clay drinking-jars and flower pots, and along the long trail made by feet walking between the nightshade bushes, which sparkled with tiny blueberries, toward Sidi Hasan Abu Tartour cemetery with its mud-brick masonry and the graves they climbed to reach the berry bushes. They'd eat the berries and fill their pockets with them, and at home, he'd get beaten because the pockets of his gallabiya would be stained with berry juice. Those tall berry bushes were filled with white and red syrup. There was Sayyid, the bald-headed boy, and the small yellow rooms on the far side, where the Ministry of Religious Endowments buildings are now, which they say Napoleon built as prisons and which Baron Meyer made into stables for the thoroughbreds he raised and raced. And the floods: the water running, overflowing, churning the red silt, rising until the entrances of the houseboats were level with the road and the gangplanks rose upward to reach the boats. The lotus plants, the ferries, the decorated boats, the whole world on the riverbank. And his father taking his hand and watching the sluggish whirlpools that roiled and collected the flotsam and spun it around, sucking and submerging it into its angry vacuums. Amir thought about how the whirlpools cleaned the surface of the water.

He began to become aware that something strange was happening, then after a moment pinpointed the cause: what he was hearing over the loudspeaker wasn't the Qur'an at all. Sheikh Hamada al-Abiad must have finished his recitations, since what he heard was a voice mumbling, "you're talking bullshit." A short period of silence passed, then the voice returned and said that they probably didn't know who the Baron Henri Meyer was: he used to own Imbaba back when it was all just cantaloupe fields. Amir heard the sound of something heavy being dragged along the ground and a loud scraping noise. All the while, the voice went on about how in the past anybody could just stretch out his hand, grab a cantaloupe, and eat it without anyone noticing. But, the voice said, he never did that because those who ate Imbaba's cantaloupes would invariably get the runs. This was a well-known fact. It was even established in history books that when the French Army came from Umm Dinar to set up camp nearby and do battle with Murad Pasha of Murad Street fame, they ate the local cantaloupe. And it's written somewhere when Napoleon saw his army afflicted with diarrhea, he ordered them not to eat the local melons. They could eat cantaloupe from anywhere but Imbaba. And the savants of the French Expedition proclaimed that whoever wanted to eat Imbaban cantaloupe had to boil it in water first. They weren't allowed to eat it without taking that precaution.

Right then, Amir recognized the voice on the loudspeaker. It was Amm Omran. Amir turned to look at those who were sitting in front of the café. He saw that many of them had become aware of what was going on. He smiled and his eyes met those of Faruq and Shawqi. Amm Omran's tired voice came blaring over the loudspeaker hung on the front edge of the building, and Amir heard him saying that one day, way back when, Hagg Awadullah arrived from his distant village while we were in the market. He was short and skinny and didn't resemble any of his children. Amir sort of looks like him, if you look at him real closely. The Hagg worked for the Baron, collecting money from the peasants who rented land and grew cantaloupe on it. And the Hagg would give the money to the Baron. Sometime afterwards, the Baron built Kit Kat, which you know of, and leased it to Khawaga Kaloumirous. A young child cried, and Amir heard Umm Abduh patting the child's back with her hand while saying, "Hoooooo." But then two other crying voices exploded. Amm Omran said that when the khawagas brought the materials to build Kit Kat, Hagg Muhammad Musa, Sheikh Hosni's father, got some men together and began to steal wood, bricks, and limestone. Everyday, they'd steal just a little so that the Baron and the khawagas wouldn't notice. Hagg Awadullah knew what was going on, but didn't say anything. We saw Kit Kat grow and grow, and that building was growing right with it—that ancient little structure that Maallim Sobhi bought—that building, which you've never liked, which no one's ever liked, was built with bricks and mortar of the highest quality. The roof supports were oak, the banisters, the doors, the windows made from precious wood that smelled like musk, the stairs, the floors of the reception hall, the impressive oak chairs, the authentic white marble, the stained glass windows. You could say that the building and the Kit Kat Club were made from the same mold, although this is a small building. Yet when you walk by it, it smells exactly like an open vial of sweet ambergris. And this is Kit Kat with its "dancing and drumming and kings and ministers and singing." Hagg Muhammad Musa said that this house belonged to him even though he'd stolen the materials for building it. When they confronted him, he said that he hadn't really stolen them, but had just appropriated them. He wasn't afraid of anybody and would talk about how those who'd built Kit Kat were the real thieves. He was simply taking his fair share and wouldn't prevent anyone from doing the same. Especially since the materials were going to build a huge nightclub that served alcohol.

Hagg Awadullah didn't tell the Baron. Instead he opened a small grocery store in the building. Hagg Muhammad Musa never collected rent from him. But the grocery store didn't do so well, and he transformed it into Awadullah's café. The Nubians used to love to sit there. They worked in Kit Kat, then they'd come to the café and drink tea with milk. Nubians love tea with milk better than anything else. And Hagg Awadullah became the chief sheikh in the area.

Amir realized that everyone sitting at the café had turned to look at him, at the place which had become so silent. Not a word. Not a domino clacking or die being thrown. In the middle of the road, between the café and the mosque, Abdullah was standing, his hands in the pockets of his tattered apron, his head bending backward looking toward the blaring loudspeaker. Galal, the juice vendor, was frozen in front of his shop, a machete in his right hand, a dessicated piece of sugar cane in his left. Maallim Husayn, the fish seller, his hair dyed brown, his face serious, was leaning on the countertop in his shop next to the entrance to the Imbaba Cinema. The group of beer-drinking young men had fallen silent at the kiosk of Khawaga who leaned out from the illuminated opening of the shack. Qasim Effendi who'd returned to his place behind the kiosk, crossed his legs.

Over the loudspeaker Usta Qadri said something unintelligible and Amm Omran disagreed, telling him that what he said could not have taken place because Amm Omran had gone off to war with Abd al-Salam at the time. "God have mercy on your soul, Abd al-Salam. He died when the Turks began to hit us with their artillery, and when I last saw him, they were putting him in a coffin. When I returned, the Army began their blessed revolution. Then they closed the Kit Kat Club, but people broke in and began to open up shops inside the place. There was Hagg Muhammad Musa al-Shami's place; Ahmad Hasan and his partner Muhammad Atiya opened their café there." Usta Qadri English threw in that a sleazy bar was opened too. Amm Omran added, "And the roaster oven where they sold seeds and nuts." It was there till the very end. Until the contractor came and tore it all down, leaving the winter hall for last so he could salvage the wood and marble. People started to pray there on Fridays. Then it was inhabited by Rabia and his children who made fishing nets. But when the contractor tore that down too, where the Kit Kat Club had once been became a huge vacant lot. Muhammad Atiya couldn't find a space to open a café. So when Hagg Awadullah happened to die that same week, Muhammad Atiya began to rent the café because Awadullah's sons had become effendis. They were educated now and didn't want to work in a café. Some time after this, an article appeared in the papers about how they'd found Kaloumirous murdered in his room at the National Hotel on Sulayman Pasha Street. The papers said that his throat had been slashed, and he was wearing a woman's dress. This was all true because Kaloumirous was in fact a khawaga and into khawaga perversions.

In those days, Sobhi was just a wandering chicken vendor, but then God blessed him with the lottery ticket and he purchased the building. Usta Qadri mumbled a few words, saying it was Sheikh Hosni who bought it. And Amm Omran said that that was indeed what happened, that the deeds of purchase fell into the lap of the blind Sheikh Hosni. But because he was so indebted to Haram, the hashish dealer, it was Haram who profited, "Yes sir. Sheikh Hosni's hash and opium habits cost him the house." Usta Qadri said, "God damn you Sheikh Hosni!" and slapped his hands together to underscore what he had said. Qadri continued, "Yes sir. Maallim Sobhi made a deal with Haram against that hash head Sheikh Hosni. Together they made him use his hash bills to sell the building." And they were going to make payments on the remainder in the form of a daily fifty piaster piece of hashish for a period of six months. "Oh yes. Haram would play a trick like that on anybody. Why, only today he tricked the police and escaped punishment. He's sitting right now with Fathiya. He stashes his drugs and his money in her house everyday, you know. You know. Fathiya. She lives over on Tawakkul Alley."

Amm Omran refused to believe the tale of how Amm Migahid had died. "No. These guys are full of shit," he said. "I'm the one who found Amm Migahid. I'm the one who left my house alone in the middle of the night and went to the shop. I saw him sitting. And he wasn't asleep. I know because when he sleeps, he sleeps on his side. The alleyway was completely empty. I was standing in the cold, saying to him, 'Greetings.' But he didn't reply at all. I was taken aback, because I still didn't know.

And I walked into the shop and put my hand on his shoulder saying, 'Why don't you answer me, Migahid?' But he fell from my hand on to his side while looking directly at me. I tried to make him sit up, like he was before, but I couldn't. That's when I knew he was dead. You were asleep. I called out to you, but you didn't answer me. You hadn't turned on the light for me.

"I went to the baker's and began to knock on the window. His wife answered, asking who it was knocking on their window this late at night. I told her that it was me. She asked me, "Do you need something this late Amm Omran?" And I said yes I do. I want you to wake up the baker because Migahid has died. She woke up the baker, and when he came out, we carried Migahid's body and put it on the wooden ful cart. The baker grabbed onto one side of the cart, and I rolled up my pajama sleeves and grabbed my side. And we went like that through the rain and night to where his family lives. When we got there, we saw them. And when we saw them, we gave them his body. The baker went home after that. As for me, I went home alone without anyone seeing me."

Suddenly, coming over the loudspeaker, there was the loud sound of someone rapping on the door. And the voice of someone asking them to turn the loudspeaker off, because, in case they didn't know it, it was still on. And because he'd heard their conversation while coming over on a ferry across the Nile from Zamalek "where there was a bunch of gunfire." Usta Qadri English cried out, "Oh my gosh!" All at once, everyone burst out laughing and the spirit of Kit Kat Square returned. Faruq got up and ran toward Fadlallah Osman Street. Coming after him, Shawqi was enthusiastically adjusting his crotch. Maallim Sobhi peered out from among his chicken crates. Sgt. Abd al-Hamid gazed directly ahead in silence. Abdullah stood still in the middle of the street. He stopped staring only when he heard with his own ears the sound of the switch shutting off the loudspeaker. He walked across the street and asked Sgt. Abd al-Hamid to give him two cigarettes, but the sergeant didn't respond. Abdullah stretched out his hand, took the cigarettes from an open pack, threw some piasters on the cart and turned away. The sergeant looked at the coins and smacked them as he said, "God have mercy on your soul, Hagg Awadullah."

Hagg Awadullah was the one who arranged that two cups of tea would find their way to him each day, on account of his being the man responsible for law and order in the neighborhood. Not that the sergeant would always drink both cups. For that reason, he kept track of how many he had on his credit with Abdullah. On this balance he was able to treat Amm Omran, Maallim Ramadan, or anyone else. He only drank one cup of tea during the early evening. Then he walked along Murad Street, stopping here and there, until he got to the spot and then he'd disappear inside. Before it got too late, he'd leave and return to the Kit Kat Club. If he saw the colored lanterns shining brightly in the long window, he knew that the king was there. At first, he would only glance tentatively at the small royal entrance in the wall of the rearmost hall before walking away quickly. With time, he learned to loiter a little, coughing and clearing his throat, perhaps chasing away some of the children who were trying to peer inside. After he sensed that the king had heard him, he would walk away along the narrow sidewalk, happily kicking the ground with his clean regulation boots. The old walls of the nightclub were over there. Over here was the asphalt of the quiet street, the riverbank, Zamalek, and the silent stars in the sky. He'd stop under the massive camphor tree without seeing them, the children of Qatr al-Nada and Fadlallah Osman perched on the high branches, spying. He stopped and eavesdropped on their whispered warnings among the heavy green leaves. He adjusted his rifle (that had no bullets) with its wooden butt and long barrel. He squinted and looked for the children between the jasmine vines covering the wall.

In those days he used to walk across the square. With his back to the end-of-the-line tram-stop, he looked toward the tall gate and the short trees along its sides, the open entrance between its stone columns, the pots of homegrown flowers. The faint light on the soil of the soft earth, the silent movement, unbroken save for the arrival of a dancer or stand-up comedian, who would arrive and quickly rush in. It didn't take long before he recognized their voices in the loudspeakers of the nightclub hidden amid the hosed-down green grass: the ministers, the important men of the court, the foreigners leaving the club, accompanied by women. The women wearing long gowns, having to bend their bodies carefully to fit into the interiors of the cars parked next to the guava orchard on this side of the square. The jewelry glistening on their earlobes and on their abundant white cleavage. Often, handouts were dispensed to those who worked at the entrance and to Abd al-Khaliq, the undertaker, who usually hosed down the square. He waited out there without knowing if there were any handouts in store for him or not. Then Amm Omran the cook might come out and give him some, "God reward you, Amm Omran!" He hid a number of pieces of grilled meat under his overcoat, and he'd accompany Amm Omran until Qatr al-Nada, take his share of the food and leave him entering Amm Migahid's shop where they would sit until daybreak. Then the sergeant would go off to "the spot."

Some nights Amm Omran would emerge with half a bottle or more of cognac. The two of them would forget Amm Migahid, head toward the building and the sergeant would climb up to the wooden tower with Amm Omran. During the summer, Amm Omran loved to sit out on the roof in the large chair that Khawaga Kaloumirous gave him when the king praised a dish of grilled meat that he had cooked. Originally, the chair had belonged to the Baron Henri Meyer who gave it to the khawaga when he came to visit him in his palace with a troupe of foreign dancing girls. Hagg Awadullah used to say that the chair tossed away on Omran's roof was the favorite chair of the Baron and that he'd heard the Baron say that since he'd let the chair slip out of his possession, he was no longer able to sit in peace or hold a thought. The chair was made from pitch pine, whose fragrance helped one to think clearly. Amm Omran himself said that although this was true, the narrow door to his apartment wasn't wide enough to bring it in from the elements. For that reason, he had left it on the roof until he could find a way to move it inside. But in the winter, the sergeant would join Amm Omran in his wooden room. While they ate, Amm Omran got drunk and gossiped about the political secrets and scandals of the ruling class. The sergeant used to love the strange things that came out when Omran started talking. And he loved to stay and listen. But each time, Amm Omran's voice would begin to fade and waver slowly between the wooden walls. He would start talking about the date trees he planted with his sister who disappeared when she was a child. And Bab Zuwayla. And the old water ducts. The sergeant would almost lose himself beside Amm Omran and forget to make his rounds. At that moment, he'd leave Omran reading his foreign newspapers, smoking the pipe that he kept in the upside-down white hat on the large wooden radio and drinking what was left of the cognac. Leaving the tower, he went to the spot where he stayed until they heard the dawn call to prayer. They'd walk over to the small mosque on the riverbank. Zein the boatman would perform the call to prayer and Sheikh Hosni would be the imam. It was only during the month of Ramadan that they regularly came to pray at dawn. When they returned down Murad Street, he'd leave them and walk by himself along the riverbank until he reached the police station where he'd turn in his rifle and visit the regulation toilet. Then he'd go home to sleep. The sergeant wanted to sleep right now, "God reward you, Amm Omran." He lit a cigarette for himself and turned around.

It began to rain and the first drops pattered noisily on a piece of paper discarded in the gutter.

Chapter
Twelve

THE GREAT HARAM jumped to his feet. Amm Omran had scandalously exposed him over the microphone. And now the authorities—and everyone else for that matter—knew where he hid his provisions, "Dammit! He's really got me in deep shit!"

Sliding his feet into his shoes, he murmured to Fathiya, "I have to go now."

"Take your stuff with you."

The Great Haram took a small pillowcase and threw all his drugs and money inside. He hurried out of the apartment and went down the stairs without making a sound.

Gaber jumped over the countertop and onto his black bike with the big metal basket. He sped out of the alleyway until he passed the café.

Khawaga, wearing his wool gallabiya and his Orient brand watch, walked out and put himself in Gaber's way. He grabbed Gaber and requested the pleasure of his company. He told Gaber that the beys wanted to treat him to a drink, and it'd be rude to refuse their hospitality. A group of friends had laid out a spread on the hood of one of their cars. A newspaper was unfolded and covered with pieces of cheese and bread, lettuce leaves, a handful of green and black olives, and a pile of tomato slices. On top of the refrigerator, sweating bottles of beer were neatly stacked. Khawaga looked at Gaber and smiled, showing his gold tooth. He was holding half a bottle of beer in his hand because he liked to join his customers in drinking. As he liked to say, it was nice for people to sit together. Khawaga regularly drank up the profits from his beer sales and then some. Gaber, in contrast, was never seen drinking with his customers. And it was well known that he didn't drink because it went straight to his head. On his days off, he left the shop in his mother's care and went to play a game or two of football against Mounira or the Gezira Club. Then he went with Faruq and Shawqi to eat rice with lentils and catch the late show at the cinema. He was still sitting on his bicycle, his right leg planted on the ground. His large body leaned forward, and, with his elbow, he propped himself up on the metal basket. He stared at his brown face and smiling eyes, thinking about how he wanted to get over to Zamalek to pick up the bags of milk and the cups of yogurt. As for Khawaga, he stood in the neon light hanging over the kiosk's little entrance. He wanted to trick Gaber, to tempt him, to pour a glass or two of beer for him, then to let him go back to his shop, drunk head-over-heels, a spectacle for the regulars of his place, some of whom might be then lured over to Khawaga's kiosk. He asked Gaber to dismount and have a glass of beer with them. "Try some real fresh beer."

Gaber turned his kind eyes from Khawaga's face and said that he was going to Zamalek to fetch the milk and yogurt, "Maybe another time, really. It's just that I've left the shop unattended."

Khawaga gripped the bicycle's handlebars and said, "Don't be rude. If nothing else, have a drink for the sake of those folks standing there."

One of them snickered, "Apparently, he's afraid to come down off his bike. Maybe he won't be able to get back on!"

Laughing along with them, Gaber dismounted and gave himself over to God's will. Parking the bicycle on the curb, he waved to Qasim Effendi who was sitting next to the kiosk, with his legs crossed. Gaber walked up to the bottles of beer stacked on the large refrigerator. Gleeful, Khawaga leaned over inside his kiosk to get a glass and fill it from his bottle. But Gaber reached out, raised a bottle to his mouth, bent his head backwards, and didn't lower it until the bottle was empty. He grabbed a second bottle, still unopened, and yanked off the metal cap with his teeth, letting the cap fall between his feet. In the course of just a few minutes, Gaber managed to polish off nine bottles. He wiped off his mouth with the back of his hand while grabbing his bike and saying, "No offence, Beys, but I'm sort of in a hurry." Gaber turned to Khawaga who stood speechless among the packs of imported cigarettes and said, "Thanks very much, Maallim." He jumped on his bicycle and sped across the square chuckling, "Fucking bastards think I'm a fool; they must think I'm a khawaga."

Chapter
Thirteen

ON AMM OMRAN'S way home from Usta Qadri English's, he stopped once in a while at the walls of the houses that pressed against each other. He stretched his hand out and felt the rain now falling in light drops. He made a fist, then released it and wiped his hand on the leg of his striped pajama pants. Every time he came upon the high slippery threshold of a building, he'd climb over it and lean against the wall. Just before he got to his building's entrance, a tiny bark came from near Amm Migahid's shop. Amm Omran slowly approached, stopping beneath a sloping wooden balcony. Resting a hand on his shaking knees, he bent over and found a small, shaggy puppy crouched against the wall. He stretched out his right hand and touched its wet hair, its tiny, trembling body. He picked up the dog with both hands and crossed the alleyway into the building. Holding the dog against his chest with one hand, he walked over the flooded doorstep and across the damp space in front of the ground floor room. Then he turned and began to climb the stairs.

His wooden room was in the rear of the small rooftop with its cramped, covered toilet. Amm Omran walked forward and stopped behind the large wooden chair. He looked out over the buildings' rooftops, Kit Kat Square, the large yellow Khalid ibn al-Walid mosque, and the three thoroughfares that led into the neighborhood: al-Sudan Street, al-Nil Street, and Murad Street which intersected the first two. While the dog tried to escape, grinding its sharp claws into the fabric of his flannel pajamas, he looked at the huge camphor tree, at the café and the chicken crates. He petted the dog while turning to face the other way: the flooded asphalt, the nearby river covered by a layer of light mist, the trees on the opposite bank, the bright lights in the windows, and the closed balconies of the massive Zamalek apartment buildings stretching off into the pitch-darkness of night. Then he opened the door and turned on the lights. He shut the door tight behind him.

The electric light bulb dangled on a thin, braided wire hanging from the ceiling. It was covered by a crystal shade with ornamented edges. Next to the brass four-poster bed, there was a low seat and a table with stacks of newspapers. In their midst, there stood an inlaid mother-of-pearl frame around a faded picture of a family. There was the cushion covered by worn fabric thrown on a long mattress next to the wall facing the bed and the low table. He bent down and placed the dog on the cushion. In the near corner of the apartment, next to a trunk whose sides were covered by faded travel stickers, he had arranged the kitchen utensils. He took an orange colored towel and dipped it into the water container next to an empty trashcan and a round brass pan. He walked back to the dog that was lying on its wet stomach, wagging its tail. He sat next to the dog and began to dry its long, tangled hair, removing the mud stuck in its paws. When he finished with that, he walked over to the small wicker basket and took out a chunk of bread, put some feta cheese on it, and, breaking it into small bites, he set it in front of the dog. Then, he sat on the bed and took off his black shoes, leaving his long socks on. He stood up and unbuttoned his pajama top, taking it off along with his pants. Underneath these pajamas, Amm Omran wore another pair, also of flannel with faded stripes. He walked to the door and checked the latch once again. Crossing the room and opening the rear window that looked out over the courtyard, he leaned out and saw the light in front of Gaber the grocer's. He couldn't see anything else. When he heard the voice of that young man Faruq yelling from nearby, he leaned in and shut the window. He climbed onto his big bed and lifted his legs and sat cross-legged. He began to look at the puppy. When Amm Omran saw him stand up, the flesh furrowed between his two neatly trimmed-eyebrows, and he told the dog to sit down. Every now and then, however, the dog shook himself and approached the bed in slow steps. His tail was raised in the air, and he sat on his hind legs. He looked directly into Amm Omran's toothless mouth and smiled.

Chapter
Fourteen

SHEIKH HOSNI TOOK out the pocket watch that had once belonged to his father, Hagg Muhammad Musa. He began to wind it and remembered sitting next to his mother on the couch. "See this watch? It belonged to Dad, this silver watch. I want you to pay attention to what I say, because I'm going to teach you how to tell time. That way, you can answer me when I ask you what time it is. You'll know how to look at it and read it and tell me. You listening? Okay. See this big knob in my fingers? The one exactly in the middle? Yes, that one. Do you see the two black hands inside the watch? You'll see one long one that tells the minutes, and one short one that tells the hours. I'll twist the knob upwards, like this, and the two hands spin like that. See them? They move, don't they? I want you to tell me when the two hands come together right underneath the knob. There? Are they exactly on top of each other? That means it's twelve o'clock.

"Look to the right a little and you'll find tiny little marks. They tell the minute. Then you see the marks that are a little bigger, looking like the numeral '1'? Well, it is a '1', but it's written in English. See it? Now I'm going to twist the knob slowly. See the long hand going past the short one? Tell me when it reaches the mark that looks like '1.' It's there? Really? Exactly there? That means it's 12:05. At this mark, it's ten past. Then, a quarter past. Twenty past. Twenty-five past. And like this, it's exactly half past. See how the short hand has gone almost halfway below the knob? Right? Every time the long hand has gone around the clock, the short one only moves one of these marks. Okay. Here's 12:35. Twenty till. Uh huh. Quarter till. Ten till. And five till. Then the minute hand's back at twelve. See how far the hour hand has moved? Only one mark. That's one o'clock on the dot. Correct you are!" 1:05. God have mercy on your soul, Mother."

He raised his large, hunched-over face, his long beard peppered with white hair. He sat like that in the corner of the dark room, on a worn-out yellow floor mat. Papers, empty cigarette boxes, matchbooks, dry orange peels, and dirt had piled up around him. He had been listening to Amm Omran and Usta Qadri's conversation over the loudspeaker. He changed his shirt and long underwear, smoked a cigarette, and meditated He thought about Nour and remembered how after her death the children were taken off to live with her brothers' families. And, remembering his mother and father, his tired eyelids began to tremble over their empty sockets. He brought the watch up to his ear for a moment then returned it to his inside pocket. He stood up, stretching his hands into the blackness around him. He grabbed his cane and leaned on it while he slid his feet into his sandals. His short, slight frame turned. He put out his cane and left his one-room apartment on the roof of the big building. He felt the coldness, drops of water on his shaved head, his face dangling on his skinny neck like a donkey's. He walked over to Umm Ruwayih's chicken coop and sat in front of it. Stealthily, carefully, he opened the gate and smelled the warm stench of the chickens, and heard their exaggerated movements as they tried to escape to the far corner of the cage. He stretched out his hand, feeling along the ground, until he found an egg which he snatched up and put in the outer pocket of his jacket. He closed the door to the coop and put the latch back where it had been. He walked down the rail-less staircase until Sheikh Hamada al-Abiad's apartment. Then, turning to follow the stairs, he continued his descent until he got to the door to Umm Ruwayih's room. Putting an ear to it, he listened for a moment, then raised his foot high over the doorstep and left the building.

Bathing Girl

A drizzle fell from the low clouds. Softly, it touched the surface of the river. Yusif al-Naggar could see the drops in the light of sparks flying out from the welding shops along the street. He could feel the warm rain on his cheeks. It made no noise save for a slight patter as it fell, rhythmically, and it cleansed the leaves of the castor palms so lightly, leaf by leaf. The air was filled with the smell of smoke. Roaches crawled out, scarabs scrambled here and there, and lizards crept through the rubbish along the riverbank and through the thick, wet weeds at the edge of the water. You were raised here. Remember?

Yusif stared at the crumbling stone steps, at the lights of the street reflecting pale in the river's waters. Are these the same steps? Were they the same rocks you used to sit on? He remembered a rock with a smooth, dry, clean surface. Its base was submerged in the water, covered by a green layer—slippery, like velvet. You'd sit resting your skinny yellow fishing rod on your left arm, baiting the hook with paste mixed with stale cheese or ghee. No bigger than a grain of wheat. Then you took the rod in your right hand and threw the silk line into the river's waters, which took the lead weight, sinking it in the depths nearby. You stared at the bobber floating. You watched it carefully as it drifted on the water's surface. You let out the line so as to free it from the deceptive play of the water's chop. By the time the sun rose over

Imbaba Bridge, you'd had brought in a pile of the little fry fish, and a few of the larger 'ray' fish. Girls would have already come down to the river with their mats and pans, and she was there with them. You felt her presence when she bent over, setting her load on the edge of the river here. She stood up to her ankles in the river water, gazing at the houses of Zamalek on the opposite bank. Don't you remember?

Twenty years have passed.

She walked forward and lifted her light dress. She gathered it between her thighs and held it tightly while bending over in front of you on the surface of the water. As she washed dishes, her body began to move up and down with the movement of her arms. From time to time, she lifted her face to push her loose hair from her eyes, and her warm chest would show. Your face met hers, but your eyes never did. You sat on the rock in the water. Her sudden fear about what had happened became apparent and she sighed. When she finished, when the two of you finished, she adjusted her body, put her hands on her hips and pushed her chest out, looking into the sun rising over the bridge, and squinting her large eyes. Then she bent into the river and began to bathe her body. She rubbed water over her thighs, her arms, her face. She undid an edge of the gown wrapped under her legs and let it fall lightly around her. She walked out of the river carrying the pots on her head and walked up the stone steps, her gown clinging to her wet body. Between the contours, thick drops of water fell.

That day you gathered the weeds around you and lit a fire. You wrapped up the fishing tackle, and picking out the best of the ray fish, you threw them into the little tongues of flame. You wound the line around the rod and stuck the hook into the fishing float and laid it down in the grass. You put out the fire and picked up the grilled ray. You took each one by the tail and dipped it into the river water to cool it. You ate the dorsal meat that tasted like poultry. You drank another glass of rum. You're drunk. No. You're just happy. Everyone had his own way of reeling in the hook. You liked to observe them as you fished. There were those who reeled in the rig while running, bending their rods toward the riverbank so the fish wouldn't fall back into the water, and then later, watching the part of the line dangling in the water to see if they had caught a fish. You watched them and were filled with amazement about how serious, how greedy they were. Even their memory still delights you. There were those who were even more practiced. These professionals would yank their poles in a fast, contorted jerk and the lucky fish would come out of the water on the end of the line, flying in the air, making a complete circle, its weight stretching the line out, swinging it around so that it smacked into the open left hand of the fisherman who, gripping the pole with his other hand, would use his fingers to pry the tiny hook out. You were good at this method too, although you never used it unless the fishing spot was crowded. That was because, whenever you fished this way, the children would stay away and give you more space to maneuver. And there were those who held their rod with both hands and stood up from where they sat. If there was a small fish on the line, they pulled the rig straight up and climbed the sloping bank. If nothing turned up, they would look at the end of the fishing line, appearing to be distracted by something else and then go to look for a new place to fish, perhaps only a step or two away. Maybe they would grab their pole and go to another fishing spot, or maybe they wrapped their tackle around their pole, climbed the bank and went home. When the riverbank was empty, you fished in the way you liked most. You pulled the pole once, gently, leaving the slack in the water, until you felt, along your whole arm, the weight of a small hooked fish, resisting, pulling slowly into the depths of the river. Then you dragged it in.

You were better than those who carried their poles up and down the banks, and you had better luck too. Why don't you write about that? Why don't you write about how you never bought prepared tackle, about how you never owned a pole you didn't make yourself? You spent days going by Rabia's tackle shop, going through the bamboo until you found one that suited you. You brought it home and lit the portable stove. You straightened the pole in the heat of the fire, shaping it to your liking. You held it in front of you. It was perfect. Its straightness took on a resilience and luster, and when you tried it out in the empty space between the couch and the bed, the fine knots of the bamboo flashed. It was perfectly balanced in your hand. From the small metal box, you brought out silk thread wound around matchsticks. You hated to fish with nylon line, even though it was strong, because it spiraled down in the water and wasn't sensitive enough in transmitting the fish movements to the bob. You would take a piece of silk thread about the length of a floor tile. You'd stick the hook into the wood of the windowframe or doorjamb. You'd take the piece of thread, run it through the eye of the tiny steel hook and tie it in the middle. Then you'd twist the two strands and tie them to the end of the single thread one more time. At the knot, you'd attach a bit of lead, fixing it with your front teeth. You measured the length of the line against the fishing pole and tied it onto the last knot in the bamboo. After that, you attached a piece of cork at the right length, measured against the depth of the water at the fishing spot near the entrance to Hawa Alley. Now the rig was ready for fishing.

You're drunk. No. You learned that fishing depended entirely on precise timing, on when you pulled your line. You were an expert in understanding the movements of the bobber floating on the surface of the water. This was no easy feat, because even the slightest wind, if it pushed against the water's current, would rock the bobber. The wind might break the surface of the water, sending out tiny waves that grabbed the bob and played with it. Then the wind would hamper the bobber's movements, its play would double, and you'd have to recognize the real signals from the false because the bobber might move even when the fish did no more than brush up against the bait with a part of its body. The fish might be in its first stages of tasting the bait and the bobber would translate that into a series of small, diminishing strikes.

The fish might nibble the bait from the side or from behind, or even take the bait in such a way as to put itself in danger of being hooked. And you would see its nibbles continuously in the movement of the bobber, but you have to refrain from pulling on the pole, because the fish is still being cautious. Likewise, you shouldn't wait until the bait is half-eaten and the hook starts to show because the fish will become suspicious and swim away. Among all the possible signals, the true and the false, there's only one signal on the bobber: the moment the fish forgets itself, the moment when the fish understands everything, the moment the bite and the cork and your eye and your hand all become one. How many times have you been fooled and tensed your whole self, and the moment almost arrived, but the fish had finished the bait and swum away? But how many times did you seize the moment, the moment of pouncing, knowing that if you had jumped one second sooner, or delayed longer, the fish would have gotten away? This signal should become an inspiration for us all.

You're drunk. Not at all. You're thinking. You can even tell the kind of fish it is by the nibble and the movement it makes in the bobber. For example, basariya nibble on the bait in a succession of little bites, and the bob may dip up and down imperceptibly under the water. When you hook basariya, its resistance is much greater than its tiny length, and when you pull the line out, you find it hanging, pulling on the line, its small body with the three black spots arching. It goes limp suddenly, then jumps upwards, the line goes slack, then it falls, still dangling by the side of its mouth. It tenses and jumps again, perhaps escaping even if it saps its strength and worsens its wound. Basariya were what you caught the most when you fished with paste. Ray were fewer. Ray made the bobber tremble quickly, pushed it along the surface of the water. When you pulled a ray in, it dangled with the end of the line in its tiny mouth. It would continue to shiver; you could feel it trembling on the grip of the rod; you could hear it as though it were a small, wet ringing sound. Then its sleek silver body would become still and it would grow weak under the sun. Light, no weight at all in the palm of your hand. Its tail, tinged with the color of blood, quivering in your hand. Yusif al-Naggar thought that ray were just like women. He let the empty bottle of rum roll into the water. He wanted to write about something. Yes. Why don't you write, and say it all?

Because you are no longer you?

Because the river is no longer the same river?

Answering yes, he felt despondent. Because you are not you.

And what you're looking at isn't your river anymore. It's discarded dishwater.

You'll be healed the day that you pour out your heart and wet your lips with it. . . .

But you're content enough with the salt of tears in your mouth. And the taste of alcohol and thirst.

Yusif al-Naggar was roused by the sound of a distant explosion.

Poor Abdullah

Abdullah entered the café. He sat in one of the chairs and ordered a cup of tea for himself. "Really, Abdullah. You've been unlucky all your life." He saw the pool of mud and water that Sheikh Hosni had left in the doorway, and he remembered Nour. There wasn't a man who wasn't in love with her. Maallim Atiya, Usta Sayyid, Qasim, and everybody. Even the young men and the schoolboys were in love with her. But none of them loved her like you.

You even loved the sheikh because she was in love with him. She used to put on her skin-tight negligée and dance for him while he strummed his lute and sang, *Since You Have Decided* and *What Was Written* to her. She would sit in his lap kissing his face right in front of you. You'd serve them all night long, then you'd leave them and go home, alone. Sheikh Hosni, who was blind, saw his sweetest days with Nour. This goddamn world. You went over there to catch a glimpse of her from afar, and you'd see her lean over Sheikh Hosni when he left the house, and she'd plead with him to come home early that day. He wore his blue suit, his pressed shirt, his smart tie, his black hair parted neatly, his clean-shaven face. He sat here with his legs crossed, and you brought him black coffee without his having to order it, and you watched him, admiring him because Nour was married to him and was in love with him. He seemed larger than life to you, "In spite of the fact that he was really nobody." You worshipped him in front of everybody, and you were at his beck and call even after she died.

It's true. "You've been unlucky all your life, Abdullah." You worked as the seeing-eye dog for a blind man. You hunted blind men so he could get rich. Now he could be seen in his old clothes, begging in Agouza, Doqqi, and neighborhoods even further off. He recalled the days when luck was on their side, when they prospered, when the sheikh was blessed with the friendship of three or four blind men at once. Those days you came home late at night stoned and sat on the mat on the floor. You sat deep in contemplation until daybreak. You were thinking about whether the time had come to leave the café, to free yourself up for this other line of work. Thinking that you should be able to move freely, to hunt for blind men everywhere, from Sidi Hasan to Sidi Ismail and Mounira and the public housing and the Ministry of Public Endowment buildings, even all the way to al-Warraq!

Abdullah drifted off to sleep and imagined himself walking through a huge field, as wide as the world itself and carpeted with green herbage. He was gathering a few thousand blind men and driving them with a long stick to where Sheikh Hosni waited behind his desk, waiting to trick them and make them believe that he could see. And he was entering everything into his ledgers. It's true, "You've been unlucky all your life, Abdullah." Then the sheikh stood up, "No, don't say, 'You've been unlucky all your life,' say, 'You've been a fool all along!'" Abdullah woke up to see Abd al-Nabi, the gimp, who worked behind the counter at the café. He was drying his hands on the edge of his gallabiya and collecting his daily wage, putting it in his pocket and smiling politely at the two of them: "Until our paths cross again, Maallim Atiya. Sweet dreams, Abdullah."

Abdullah knew that tonight he wouldn't have to sweep the café. He wouldn't bring the chairs inside. The maallim wouldn't be a stickler about him preparing everything, or about him collecting all the cups, plates, chairs, tables, hookah pipes (big and small), and the tiny aluminum spoons. The maallim wasn't going to do that because a cart was coming to move it all away, just as it was. Abdullah thought that the maallim would want to collect everything from him like on any other night, but tonight of course he would take it all and put it in the cart. He would count up the earnings and the tokens one by one. He would take the money from him and count it. Once. Twice. Three times. The piaster coins by themselves. The larger change by itself. The paper currency by itself. The maallim would give Abdullah his daily wage, or what was left of it, only after deducting the customers' debts. You see, Abdullah kept a running tab with some people. He'd bring them tea and water pipes knowing full well that they weren't going to pay that day. On the days that his earnings dwindled down to a piaster or so, he got angry at the moment of reckoning, but the maallim would answer by saying, "Just let them not pay! What's the problem? You're better off than they are!" And Abdullah would say, "But what should I say to someone who just wants to drink a cup of tea or smoke a waterpipe? Should I say no? How can you say that when you know he's unemployed or broke or whatever?" Tonight, however, he wouldn't have to say that. He wouldn't unfasten his apron and hang it behind the counter because he wouldn't be coming back here. Abdullah grew tired of thinking, he wanted to leave the café, now empty save for the stacked tables and chairs. Before the cart arrived to carry off everything, he wanted to go just as he was, with the apron, the night's intake and tokens in his pocket. He wanted to leave, knowing that he wasn't going to return. He rose to go home, but Maallim Atiya stood up from behind the open box into which he was arranging the glasses and left over supplies. Limping, he rushed after him and grabbed Abdullah by the shoulders and, dragging him inside, let him go again. "Not yet, Abdullah."

Abdullah went to the disconnected refrigerator and pulled out a large, serrated ice pick they used during the summer. He attacked the Maallim who ran into the corner, "Please Abdullah, I'm you're buddy! For the sake of the beloved Prophet!" Abdullah struck him on the head with the blunt edge so as not to kill him. He struck him so hard that his whole arm vibrated. Bloodied, the maallim fell over and quickly passed out. Abdullah looked at him and became fascinated by how easy it had been. He was astounded. He had been fooled. He realized that hitting the head of a maallim could be the easiest thing in the world. Easier than work. Easier than fetching things for customers. Easier than cleaning a waterpipe. Easier than being unemployed. Abdullah walked out into the street, hallucinating, hearing voices. Still clutching the serrated metal ice pick, he walked toward Murad Street. He thought once again: what a fool he'd been.

Handprints of Blood

Abd al-Hamid saw a group of men pulling the roped calf and slaughtering it in the doorstep of the empty café. He didn't bother to get up from where he was sitting. The sergeant emptied the little change box and put the coins in the pocket of his old government-issue overcoat. From his other pocket, he removed a thin plastic bag, opened it and brought it to the edge of the cart. He shoved everything that was on the top of the cart into the bag. He picked up the gas lamp, its rounded glass covered by a cigarette carton. He carried it in his fingertips and placed it, along with the bag, next to his right foot. He stuck his hand into the cart and took out a large piece of oilcloth and spread it over the cart, letting the edges dangle, and tied it with a cord. He noticed that the café chair was still there. He turned toward the café and saw Maallim Sobhi's boys sticking their hands into the blood of the slaughtered calf and making handprints on the walls of the empty café, celebratory harbingers of the new order. He retreated backwards and looked at the chair again. Its padded seat filled with soft golden straw, its back a polished brown, its wide, smooth, arching backrest with the name clearly engraved: Awadullah. Abd al-Hamid bent over, put his arm under the back of the chair, lifted it onto his shoulder and let it dangle there. He carried his bag in his right hand. He was a slight man with slumped shoulders and a beard with scatterings of short white whiskers. The skin on his neck hung loosely behind the open collar of his gallabiya; his small eyes had no eyelashes. He took the road home but the gas lamp remained under the edge of the sidewalk. With its short metal body, a cigarette carton wrapped around it, the top of the cart protecting it from the raindrops. And the red light, no bigger than a seed, inside the glass.

Chapter
Fifteen

IT WASN'T A MYSTERY.

This is what Amir thought while standing silently under the huge camphor tree and staring at the old walls of Awadullah's café, now decorated with bloody handprints. Without the smoke and Abdullah and the cliques of people, the place looked strange. Maallim Sobhi kept out of the rain by standing inside the open doorway. One of his arms was folded across his chest with the hand hidden inside the opening of a white gallabiya, splattered with blood, appearing from under an open wool overcoat. He stood there. Around him were tall stacks of wooden cages padded with straw, filled with chickens, pigeons, and rabbits which made, in quick visible movements, a soft, humming noise broken only occasionally by the shrill screech of the unseen chickens. Amir looked over from where he stood and saw turkeys and sheep being herded into the café.

Under the rain, other cages were stacked next to the scales. He began to think to himself, but was interrupted again by the sound of a gray car braking next to the mosque wall. A petite woman, her hair wrapped in a white silk scarf, got out, and hurried across the street carrying an open basket. She stopped under the lamp hanging at the café entrance, next to the youngest and tallest of the Maallim's employees. He stood behind a wet, zinc-covered counter, grabbing chickens by his hand, tying their wings and weighing them on the scales while they were still alive. Then he took the chicken in his left hand, twisted its neck between his fingers, and slit its throat with the long knife he held in his right hand. He threw the chicken into a steaming barrel next to him. On the other side of the barrel, another boy, wearing a T-shirt and long underwear, took the chicken from the boiling water and deftly plucked its feathers. Then he cleaned out its insides and threw them into a nearby pile at the entrance where a pack of dogs and some stray cats had gathered. He put the gutted, denuded chicken into the woman's basket along with some others. Amir turned pale and walked away from where he was standing under the enormous camphor tree. He stepped onto the other sidewalk and walked toward the mosque wall without turning back to look at the café again. From the corner of his eye, he saw a pack of colored tissue paper inside the parked gray car, and a little plastic bird hanging under a windshield streaked with rain. Where the wall turned away, he stopped to look at the little wooden cart and thought of Sgt. Abd al-Hamid. The cart was covered by a piece of oilcloth now being washed by the rain. It was attached to the old stone lamppost by a steel chain. He looked at the chain hanging under the heavy rain that collected in the gutter. Amir patted the wet tarp covering the cart and thought that there was really no mystery in it. As the Awadullah café is your witness, it was lost because one maallim attacked another maallim and ended it all. But the attack was probably really directed against the café. No. It was directed at you. Against your world. Your exhausted, depleted world. As this mosque here is your witness. Yes. The café was nothing but the last gasp of this huge body softly passing before you as if it were a cloud pulsing with colors and shadows. Its memory would always be in your heart. But what a waste. Awadullah would die now because Abdullah was still too young. Amir smiled and thought, "Ah, and we used to believe in mermaids." Strange, he thought, that your life would stretch long enough to see all that, to witness you lose all that, and you had only just turned thirty.

No. It wasn't mysterious at all.

Chapter
Sixteen

GABER APPROACHED THE Zamalek bridge to pick up the bags of milk and cartons of yogurt. He saw riot police blocking the bridge and the Giza road. He hit the brakes and the wheel skidded noiselessly on the street's wet asphalt. He hurried back to Fadlallah Osman Street. He found only a young girl waiting in his shop, her head and upper body wrapped in an inside-out flannel gallabiya. She held an empty gas canister in one hand. He took the canister and some money from her other hand and went into the storeroom. He filled the canister and gave it back to the girl. Then he put the empty crates inside, and closed the stroreroom. He turned off the interior light and locked up his shop. He remained standing there for a moment, then got on his bike and returned to the square.

Sulayman Jr. Ruins Everything for the Great Haram

When the Great Haram, carrying his incriminating bag, hopped down the stairs into the building's foyer, he stopped himself. He stepped to exit, but then saw someone he didn't recognize at first. He jumped back and tried to stifle his heavy breathing. Haram had no time to waste. But he wouldn't be able to sneak out of this place without bumping into this fat ass that nearly blocked the door. Hiding his body, Haram craned his neck and studied the profile pressed against the shutter slats. He remained there, staring until he realized that it was Sulayman, son of Sulayman, the jeweler, who lived on Murad Street. In the darkness, a pleasant smile etched itself on Haram's face. He gently stretched out his hand and patted Sulayman's shoulders while whispering, "Good evening." At the first murmur, Sulayman began to scream in a terrified voice. The Great Haram was aghast. In the shadows he groped blindly to cover Sulayman's mouth. He whispered, "What's wrong? It's only Haram."

But Sulayman was gripped with an insane fear which made him fall over and scream out, "Please, Amm Haram! Don't hurt me, Amm Haram! You're like a father to me!"

Haram jumped onto Sulayman's chest and, grabbing him by the throat, whispered in his right ear, "Shut up, God damn you!" But Sulayman, begging for help and crying in a terrified voice, began to kick at him until the bag and its contents went sailing across the foyer. Haram heard the sound of doors and windows opening, heard feet and hands swarming into the alley and saw light flooding into the passageway. When darkness returned once again, he was hugging the ground. He jumped up and ran back and forth without finding a single pound note or piece of hashish. He couldn't find the bag nor any of its contents. He found himself alone in the short, dead-end alley and was startled to hear a sound like a bugle call bursting in his ears. Stunned and afraid, he ran like a locomotive, howling and banging on the walls around him.

Chapter
Seventeen

SHEIKH HOSNI PULLED his jacket tightly around his chest and walked forward. He stopped in the middle of the muddy street and turned around, raising his sagging head. Sniffing the air, he detected a sharp stench. He heard the pounding of distant feet. He began to walk forward until he stopped himself again. The strange smell had spread and was burning his nose. The clomp of boots running along the muddy ground became louder, until it came up right behind him, almost pushing him forward with it. He began to run toward the square, where other heavy boots pounded into the pavement, rushing to cut him off. Something exploded next to him and he was thrown to the ground. Cobblestones rained down around him, trees were falling. He began to feel dizzy; the earth was spinning beneath him. As he fell on his back, his cane flew from his hand toward the Nile road. He quickly turned onto his stomach, held on to the sidewalk, and wedged himself into the gutter. He put his arms over his head and held on tight.

Chapter
Eighteen

YUSIF HEARD THE gunshots and the exploding tear gas bombs. He climbed the riverbank and saw the foul smoke blocking the entrances to Imbaba, but he wasn't able to see exactly where the soldiers were. He saw bright flashes reflecting across the other side of the square and thought at first that they were bayonets on the rifles. When he drew closer to the edge of the bank, he noticed that these flashes came from the Plexiglas face on their riot shields. He retreated to the entrance of a houseboat nearby. He sat on the squat stone wall and began to watch the square.

The Battle of the Calf's Head

"If I were to die right now, I'd be a happy man. Nay. My heart has become like stone. When I strike it, my hand it injures." Usta Qadri English shut the old volume and put it on the window sill next to the head of the bed.

Ever since Amm Omran left and Ibn al-Disuqi came to haul the loudspeaker equipment away, he had wanted to sleep. But to no avail. What had brought that animal Zaghlul into his home under the pretense of mourning Amm Migahid? He began to despair, unable to find a single excuse that would absolve that bitch Umm Abduh. He nodded and said that the truth had become clear. He got out of bed, put his coat over his house gallabiya, and wrapped a scarf around his head and cheeks until nothing showed except his angry eyes and the scruffy tips of his white mustache. He snuck out of the room, down the few stairs, and walked into the building's foyer. He was just stepping outside when gunshots and bomb blasts began to explode. He ran back into the foyer, unraveled the scarf and exposed his face. Umm Abduh walked into the doorway of their apartment asking, "What was that explosion?" She stood over the short staircase and beat her chest with her hand, "In the name of God, the Most Merciful and Compassionate! I thought you were asleep!"

Usta Qadri stood firm and motioned for her to go back inside. He wanted her to leave him alone so that he could stand there for a while, then go back inside as if he'd gone over to the café and come back. But the woman wouldn't move. The sound of explosions jolted the air around them and Umm Abduh said, "What a catastrophe! Those are canons they're firing!" She looked at his face and broke into a smile. Motioning with her hand, she said knowingly, "Okay. I'm going in."

The Usta began to fume angrily in the foyer. Now he understood that it was a decisive moment: he had to go outside or risk shame. He shot out into the street like a torpedo, and, smelling the peppery stench, he hurled himself alongside the other young men, toward the square where a cloud of smoke hovered. The darkness was ignited by another round of gunfire while he ran, watching the government troops. The soldiers fired their rifles while dodging the rocks hurled at them from all directions. He saw young Faruq, Shawqi, his son Abduh, and Gaber the grocer leading a massive group of young men, picking up the tear gas bombs which the soldiers had thrown and which spewed forth that horrible smoke. They were picking them up and throwing them back at the soldiers. Usta Qadri went crazy and began to hallucinate the words of Macbeth: "Hang out our banners on the outward walls; The cry is still, 'They come!' our castle's strength will laugh a siege to scorn." What was this sound coming from him? The of a constipated motor? Usta Qadri saw himself transformed into a fighter jet, a flying machine gun finding its ammunition in piles of rocks. He began to strafe the government troops, circling, soaring high over the mosque's minaret so as not to collide with it. He flew through their ranks and landed safely on the shoulders of one of the soldiers and took his truncheon. He hurled himself like a tornado sweeping over the edges of the square in direct and bloody combat. During all this, he happened to overturn Zaghoul's cart, climbing over its broken pieces triumphantly. He made a complete circle until he saw himself in front of the café. He was completely beside himself, but managed to notice that although there were no people there, it was packed with chicken crates. He noticed Sheikh Hosni lying in the gutter, his head under his arms. He began to approach the body. He hesitated, until his nerves calmed. Then he saw the Sheikh stretch his hand along the asphalt and quickly pull it back. The Usta was astonished because he'd assumed that the Sheikh was dead. He seized the opportunity and ran over to him, grabbing him under the armpits to lift him. Sheikh Hosni jolted and screamed, "Who are you?"

"It's Qadri."

"Qadri who?"

"Usta Qadri, man!"

Qadri tried to pull him away from the battlefield, but Sheikh Hosni began to scream, "My cane! My cane!"

Usta Qadri said, "What cane? Right now? The cane's gone."

"Gone? How? It's right over there. Look."

"Give me a break. Let's go. Or should I go and leave you here?"

"I can't move without my cane."

Usta Qadri wanted to get out of there, but the sheikh was grabbing onto him. Qadri yelled at him, "Okay. Get your hands off my throat. I'll go look for it."

"I'm going with you! Take me with you!"

Usta Qadri tried to pull himself away, cursing this horrible coincidence under his breath. But there was no way out. He walked toward the cane. Sheikh Hosni was hanging from his neck. When Qadri leaned over and grabbed the cane, Sheikh Hosni cried out, "Give it!" For an instant the sheikh had both his hands on the cane as he asked, "Where are we now?"

"In front of the goddamn gate," Usta Qadri said, and just then, another series of gunshots and explosions went off and Usta Qadri English ran off. Sheikh Hosni wanted to flee too, but something hit him in the head. Blood began to flow. He let go of the cane, lifted his hands to his face, and screamed, "Oh, I'm dying! Oooooooh!"

Usta Qadri returned and hoisted the sheikh onto his shoulders. He ran back to the building with him on his back. When he saw Umm Abduh standing in the doorway, he yelled at her to bring him some water and iodine tincture. When she turned to go, he wanted to kick her, but instead just screamed at her to move and dropped his heavy load. When they went inside, she brought a pan. Sheikh Hosni sat on the sofa and Umm Abduh dabbed water over his wound, saying, "Thank God you're safe, Sheikh Hosni." He began to tell her about how the soldiers had fired bullets at him. Then he adjusted himself and slapped his hands on his thighs. He remained like that, the water, red from the blood, flowing off his head. He said, "Where's my cane! It's gone!"

Chapter
Nineteen

FROM TIME TO TIME, the sparks poured out of the little welding shops, lighting the sky over all of Imbaba with a dazzling glow that lit up the drops of rain pouring down.

When one of the canisters exploded next to the sidewalk, Yusif al-Naggar waited until its nasty smoke emptied out, then picked it up. It was black, made out of a round piece of cardboard and a lightweight metal base. It had yellow writing in English on it: "F.L. 100 — Federal Laboratories USA, 1976." Strange, Yusif thought. He saw the huge demonstration approaching from al-Sudan Street near the Shurbagi Factories. He saw the soldiers streaming out of the alleys located between the Nasser public housing blocks. They fired bullets and canisters, then retreated and disappeared. He saw thousands of rocks raining down on the soldiers from inside of Imbaba, pushing the troops back across the square. When he looked more closely at the canisters, he noticed they were of different colors and sizes. He wanted to collect one of each and put them all in his room. He thought about how surprised everybody would be when he showed them his collection. He put the empty canister in his jacket pocket and walked into the empty area between the combatants hoping to collect one specimen from each. The second he found had the same number written on it, but it was made out of white metal and looked like a can of insecticide. A little of the liquid was still in it and was made in the same year. He found a third one, of cardboard, silver with red writing "F.L. 100." He stumbled upon an intact shotgun shell. The soldiers launched these canisters at Imbaba, and the young men picked them up, still smoking, to throw them back at the troops. Yusif approached them and searched between the stones strewn about everywhere. Between someone's feet, he found another cardboard one, "C.N. 219" and a metal rocket shaped like a speedboat with pointed ends and a hollow middle. Printed on it was "C.N. 219" also. "C.N. 218" was skinnier and longer than the others; it was silver with blue writing. He filled the pockets of his jacket, thinking that now he had six, and the shell made seven. He turned the shell over in his hands. Its cover was made out of hard, red plastic. Its base was a cap of yellow brass. At the top, the plastic was pinched together. Yusif tried to rip open the seal, but his fingernails weren't strong enough. He took out the key to Magid's apartment, and carefully used its steel edge to open the shell and empty its contents into his hand. Steel buckshot fell out, tiny like cracked wheat, but heavy and black. In the middle of all the turmoil, he poured the pellets from his hand, carefully returning them to the cartridge once more. He counted each one.

The first time he was hit, he didn't feel any pain. When the flash of light burst, it imprinted a fiery image in his eyes.

The Sheikh Gets his Cane Back

The sheikh jumped up.

He left Usta Qadri English's house and stretched out his hand, his palms turned to the ground. He headed carelessly for the square. He went from Qatr al-Nada toward Murad Street and walked until the edge of the square, his big ears catching the sound of young men moving near the walls. He turned his back on the mosque, knowing that behind him was the large stone entrance to Kit Kat. With his first step, he sensed that silence had descended upon everything. Amassed behind him, the young men defending the entrances to Imbaba had stopped talking. The government troops' were stopped in their tracks on the other side of the square. He began to kick the rocks and empty canisters and bullets that littered the ground. Then he came to a halt. It was here that he had been standing with Usta Qadri. It was here that he'd been grazed in the head by the government bullet. He took one solid step, then leaned over. He put out his right hand, letting it hang, spread in the cold air. He began to move it lightly over the ground, like he was warming himself under the thin drops of rain in the middle of the square. Suddenly, he retracted his hand and stopped. He let it dangle slack, his fingers coming closer to the ground, finally touching the cold, wet asphalt of the road. The palm of his hand came to rest on the polished handle he knew so well. He grabbed the cane and stood up. He turned and followed his cane to the back edge of the square. He stopped at the door of his building and raised his droopy head. A thin line of blood flowed from behind his big black ear. He lifted the cane above him, feeling it under the streams of rain, which was now falling heavily. He grabbed it again and, before pushing the cane to enter the building, he patted his outside pocket and smiled to himself.

They hadn't even broken the egg.

Chapter
Twenty

Yusif al-Naggar avoided looking at his wound. The fabric of his pants was torn and drenched in blood and mud. His knee looked smashed and swollen. But you got here on your own two feet, he thought. You can return to the river once again. Remember?

He looked at the opposite bank eroded by the reinforced embankments under the casinos and nightclubs. He raised his face toward the enormous steel cranes towering over him from the sky, their long extended arms and their red eyes encircling him in the heart of night. He wanted to write everything down. To write a book about the river, the children, the angry crowds taking revenge on the storefront windows, and the trees along the Nile road and the advertisements for products and films. Say that you saw them with your own eyes setting fires. And that everything, even the green river weeds, responded to them. Write that you walked on the carpets of glass covering the city and its sidewalks. Say that eyeglasses were crushed over the eyes of men, that even the vanity mirrors in girls' purses were broken, that if a young man were to have taken the mirrors, the river would have parted for him. Write about the café and Omran and everybody. Write about the world of insomnia, the smoke, the trees at night, and the little birds. The afarit of Imbaba. The tiny man who was two inches tall and whose inch-long beard was made of soft gold, red, green, and yellow straw. The tiny men who nested there in the branches of the huge camphor tree, raising a light commotion, chirping like old birds, jumping from one branch to another in their short gallabiyas which left their calico underwear and twisted legs bare. Eating the leaves and whispering their nasty little secrets to one another, secrets which they keep hidden in their flowing, multicolored beards. Laughing sarcastically, pissing on the young children and passersby. The world of the alleyway and black shawls, the arching eyebrows, the laughing eyes, the soft golden thigh at the bottom of the stairwell, the ground floor room shut tight. And Fatma, the thirsty throat that could not be quenched by your nocturnal trips seeking a drink of water. Fatma whose thirst can only be quenched by the river.

Imbaba, that sad, adulterous woman.

You're drunk.

No, you're just wounded.

He brought his body down over the slimy filth of the riverbank, smelling the stench mixed with the clean scent of the rains. Yusif approached the water. He wanted to wash his wounds.

Cleanse yourself.

How many times I drank her effervescent waters and thick silt.

Cleanse yourself.

How many times I put myself under, naked. How many times did the current take you?

The wet leaves spreading in the air emitted a light lead-colored glow. There, a distant window was open. A hanging window from which a lone human figure looked out. Behind it, a backdrop of solid light. Around it, a frame made of night.

A Departure

The explosions abated, the thick cloud of smoke dissipated. Even though rain continued to fall, the foul smell still hung in the air. His eyes filled with tears, Amm Omran sat in the large chair on the tiny rooftop terrace, a thick wool blanket thrown over his shoulders. Pushed back by the young men of Imbaba, the riot police had abandoned the nearby roads and regrouped far from the wet square, now empty except for the rocks, tear gas canisters, and bullets. The young men occupied the streets of their neighborhood and were sitting in the doorways of the buildings, leaning against walls, exchanging whispered remarks and laughing.

The two lines of the roof's low, stone wall bent to meet at the bare, wooden flagpole, which made the whole terrace look like an ark. An ark with Amm Omran enthroned at the helm. He looked out from where he sat and saw the troops on the distant shore, the Imbaba men crowded on the sidewalks that the troops had abandoned. He wanted to lift his hand and wave to them, but couldn't. He turned his face to the river until he began to doze and dreamed that the Apocalypse had begun. He imagined that the herald was crying for humanity to rise up and present themselves before the Lord Almighty. Wrapping the blanket around him, he dreamed he left the place and headed to where the congregation was gathered at Kit Kat Square. He saw people gliding down from heaven in groups and alone. He saw Maallim Sobhi emerging from hell, sitting on the curb and exhaling smoke from his nostrils and ears. He saw the specter of Amm Migahid seated on one side of a scale, measured against his deeds which were set on the other. Afraid, Amm Omran hurried away and urinated behind the mosque wall, then began to look out from there. It didn't take long before he saw Faruq take Shawqi and flee. He rushed behind them until he found himself in Awadullah's café. He drank a cup of fenugreek and talked for a while with Hagg Awadullah who was wearing a wool cloak, preparing to leave. He drank another glass of cognac and settled further into the large wooden chair. His eyes cracked open slightly. When he spied the river, he closed them again. He began to sail off into the night and disappeared among the sparse, low-lying winter stars.

Some Rain

The drops of rain fell heavy and warm. On the surface of the river, each drop made a ripple, each one splashed upwards, then dropped, like a small pearl, glistening. In the heart of silence, he heard nothing but the regular rhythm of rain on the rooftops and the rustle of trees being cleansed on the river's edge. Sometime later, a strong northern wind descended and blew the streams of rain far away to the edge of the night. Over the edge of the dark steel bridge, the light of dawn began to show itself.

A Return

In the outside room overlooking the courtyard, Yusif al-Naggar opened his eyes slightly. The soft morning light came through the shutter slats. The empty round canisters, the different colored canisters became visible, as did the large picture on the wall. Before he closed his eyes again, he touched his new wound with his fingers.

And opened the door.

The night was over. The calm that had prevailed, like these dreams, began to retreat.

Glossary

afarit (sing. *ifrit)*: demons.

***al-Ahram*:** government daily newspaper, along with *al-Akhbar* and *al-Gumhuriya*.

Amm: literally 'uncle'; used to refer to men, in either a sarcastic or friendly manner.

basbusa: pastry made of flour, butter, sugar, and oil.

bey: derived from a Turkish title of nobility, rough equivalent of 'count,' but in modern times a form of address, which, depending on tone, can be playful, respectful, or sarcastic.

Biladi, biladi: literally 'my country, my country'; the opening words of the Egyptian national anthem.

Effendi: title of respect, used like 'Sir' or 'Mr.,' particularly for an educated man or a man who wears western clothes.

fitir: heavy, filo-like Egyptian pastry served sweet or savory.

ful: mashed fava beans, a staple of Egyptian breakfasts.

gallabiya: Egyptian name for the traditional robe.

Hagg: literally, one who has made the pilgrimage, but more commonly a general term of respect for an older man.

Khawaga: form of address for Westerners and Christians, which in the post-Nasser era usually carries disparaging connotations.

Maamur: police commissioner.

maassil: tobacco treated with molasses used in waterpipes.

Maallim: working-class form of address for uneducated, non-professional merchants, speculators, businessmen, and the bosses of local gangs of thugs.

mulid: in popular Islam or eastern Christianity, a festival celebrating the memory of a holy figure.

Shahada: Creed for attesting to belief in Islam: There is no god but God and Muhammad is his Prophet.

Sheikh: term of respect for an elderly man or patriarch; in Egypt the title is often associated with religious clerics, Sufi masters, and Qur'anic reciters.

Umm: 'Mother' or 'mother of'. It is polite and customary to address a parent by his or her eldest child's name, preceded by 'father of' or 'mother of,' for example, 'Umm Abduh.'

Usta: skilled manual laborer, particularly in transportation.

Ustaz: literally 'professor,' but used as a respectful form of address for any educated man.

Modern Arabic Literature
from the American University in Cairo Press

Ibrahim Abdel Meguid *Birds of Amber*
No One Sleeps in Alexandria • *The Other Place*
Yahya Taher Abdullah *The Mountain of Green Tea*
Leila Abouzeid *The Last Chapter*
Yusuf Abu Rayya *Wedding Night*
Ahmad Alaidy *Being Abbas el Abd*
Idris Ali *Dongola: A Novel of Nubia*
Ibrahim Aslan *The Heron* • *Nile Sparrows*
Alaa Al Aswany *The Yacoubian Building*
Hala El Badry *A Certain Woman* • *Muntaha*
Salwa Bakr *The Wiles of Men*
Hoda Barakat *Disciples of Passion* • *The Tiller of Waters*
Mourid Barghouti *I Saw Ramallah*
Mohamed El-Bisatie *Clamor of the Lake* • *Houses Behind the Trees*
A Last Glass of Tea • *Over the Bridge*
Fathy Ghanem *The Man Who Lost His Shadow*
Randa Ghazy *Dreaming of Palestine*
Gamal al-Ghitani *Zayni Barakat*
Tawfiq al-Hakim *The Prison of Life*
Yahya Hakki *The Lamp of Umm Hashim*
Bensalem Himmich *The Polymath* • *The Theocrat*
Taha Hussein *The Days* • *A Man of Letters* • *The Sufferers*
Sonallah Ibrahim *Cairo: From Edge to Edge* • *The Committee* • *Zaat*
Yusuf Idris *City of Love and Ashes*
Denys Johnson-Davies *The AUC Press Book of Modern Arabic Literature*
Under the Naked Sky: Short Stories from the Arab World
Said al-Kafrawi *The Hill of Gypsies*
Sahar Khalifeh *The Inheritance*
Edwar al-Kharrat *Rama and the Dragon* • *Stones of Bobello*
Betool Khedairi *Absent*
Ibrahim al-Koni *Anubis*
Naguib Mahfouz *Adrift on the Nile* • *Akhenaten, Dweller in Truth*
Arabian Nights and Days • *Autumn Quail* • *The Beggar*
The Beginning and the End • *The Cairo Trilogy: Palace Walk,*
Palace of Desire, Sugar Street • *Children of the Alley*
The Day the Leader Was Killed • *The Dreams* • *Echoes of an Autobiography*
The Harafish • *The Journey of Ibn Fattouma* • *Khufu's Wisdom*
Life's Wisdom • *Midaq Alley* • *Miramar* • *Naguib Mahfouz at Sidi Gaber*
Respected Sir • *Rhadopis of Nubia* • *The Search* • *The Seventh Heaven*
Thebes at War • *The Thief and the Dogs* • *The Time and the Place*
Wedding Song • *Voices from the Other World*